One second there was only air and the next, Venus's lips were brushing against his.

Something seemed to crackle and hiss between them.

Trevor had no idea how this had mushroomed so quickly. Instead of offering comfort, he was taking it. He found himself cupping the back of her head as the friendly kiss morphed into a great deal more.

Pleasure streaked through him. And though his head spun, he was acutely aware of his surroundings.

He was aware of drawing her closer to him. Aware of the tantalizing way her body touched his, setting the tranquil, cool morning on fire.

He was aware of deepening the kiss, slowly, so that she wouldn't pull away.

Most of all, he was aware of wanting to do more than just kiss her.

He was aware of wanting her.

Dear Reader,

Hi, nice to see you again. This is the second installment of KATE'S BOYS. This time around, we meet one of the triplets. Trevor Marlowe is the sensitive one, the quiet, patient one who grieved the most for his mother when she died. Consequently, Trevor hasn't been willing to risk his heart and the possibility of being hurt again. Oh, he tried once, but because he held so much of himself in check, the relationship didn't work out. And when it didn't, he felt vindicated for keeping his emotions under wraps.

But the night he comes to a strange woman's rescue changes all that. Diving into the water, he risks his life to save hers. When she first comes to, the woman his brothers refer to as Trevor's mermaid has no memory of herself or the life she led before she was pulled out of the ocean. He dubs her Venus because she came from the sea, and finds himself falling in love with a woman who might very well break his heart in the end. He has no choice but to risk it.

I hope you like this latest story of Kate Marlowe's sons and, as ever, I wish you someone to love who loves you back. Thank you for reading.

With affection,

Marie Ferrarella

USA TODAY BESTSELLING AUTHOR

MARIE FERRARELLA

THE BRIDE WITH NO NAME

SPECIAL EDITION®

Published by Silhouette Books

America's Publisher of Contemporary Romance

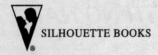

SILHOUETTE BOOKS

ISBN-13: 978-0-373-24917-6
ISBN-10:   0-373-24917-9

THE BRIDE WITH NO NAME

Visit Silhouette Books at www.eHarlequin.com

Printed in U.S.A.

Selected Books by Marie Ferrarella

MARIE FERRARELLA

This *USA TODAY* bestselling and RITA® Award-winning author has written more than one hundred and fifty books for Silhouette, some under the name Marie Nicole. Her romances are beloved by fans worldwide. Visit her Web site at www.marieferrarella.com.

To Chris, Kenny, Pat, Lori, Danny,
Edwin, Nick, Theo, Robbie, Mark, Carlos #2
and all the other rats!!

And to Carlos Aguilar and Ricky Castro,
the leaders of the Rat Pack.
From Jessi's mom

Chapter One

He was alone on the beach.

He'd hoped he would be. But despite the fact that it was almost midnight and officially one day into autumn, because this was Southern California, there was always a chance that a pair of lovers would be out, making use of the solitude.

Either a pair of lovers or a homeless person, seeking a little uninterrupted sleep on one of the benches that outlined a portion of Laguna Beach.

Half beach, half park, with a carefully crafted pseudo-Mediterranean backdrop in the distance, this particular section offered the best of both worlds, which was why, when he'd decided to finally take the plunge and open up his own restaurant, Trevor Marlowe had chosen this area for his locale.

The windows of his restaurant, Kate's Kitchen, looked out onto the sea. There were times when he thought his patrons came as much for the view of the Pacific as they did for the cuisine, but Kate, his stepmother and the restaurant's namesake, was quick to set him straight. She insisted that he cooked rings around anyone she knew. Considering he had acquired his love of cooking and learned to create culinary magic from her, Kate's words were high praise indeed.

Not that Kate was actually capable of saying anything even remotely negative, he thought now with a smile. Hurting feelings just wasn't in her nature; it never had been.

Kate Llewellyn Marlowe was kind. Kind, loving and nurturing, with just enough feistiness to prevent her from being sweetly dull. She kept things around her constantly moving. It was she who encouraged him to follow his dream, she who slipped him money on those occasions when he was short so that he could go on to that culinary academy in Italy. She'd supported him as he perfected skills that were already considerable.

Kate had turned out to be the best influence in all their lives—his, his three brothers' *and* his father's. He'd hate to think where all of them would be today if his harried father hadn't stumbled across Kate, armed with puppets, working a children's party. According to the story, his father had instantly sensed that this was the woman who could handle his overenergized brood.

He and his brothers had been a handful, acting out, mostly because of their bereavement over the recent death of their mother. There was no telling where he, Mike,

Trent and Travis might have wound up had there been no Kate. Possibly juvenile hall.

But, thank God, Kate had come into their lives, bringing sunshine and patient understanding as well as her puppets.

Now Trevor believed that all of them would have been lost without her.

Had that really been twenty years ago? he marveled. It hardly seemed that long.

One long wave made it out farther than its brethren, soaking his bare feet before receding. He felt the sand eroding beneath his soles, the water symbolically trying to draw him as it retreated to the ocean.

He'd better start heading back, Trevor thought, though he made no immediate effort to turn around. He allotted himself a couple more minutes. He really did need to unwind. It had been a long, hard week and the weekend hadn't even arrived yet.

From where he stood, tomorrow wasn't overly promising. Without anyone calling in sick, he was already short one set of hands. That meant double duty for him until he could get a temp agency to send him a replacement for his salad girl. Thinking of the incident caused him to frown.

His previous salad girl, Ava, had quit, not because of any problems at work but because her boyfriend, a biker whose upper torso was all but covered with tattoos, wanted to go on a two-month road trip. Ava couldn't bear the idea of being without him for so long. So, amid profuse apologies this afternoon, she'd removed her apron and then just taken off.

But he'd handle it, Trevor thought. Somehow, he always did. Kate's influence had taught him that he could do anything if he set his mind to it.

He sighed. Sometimes the credo was harder to live by. Which was why he was out here now, after closing time, walking off some steam and maybe just a small amount of anxiety.

Trevor waited for the calm to come. It was obviously taking its time.

He realized that he'd stopped moving and stared out into the endless ocean. The full moon drew a long, almost white streak along the water. It trailed along like the tail of a kite. The night was so quiet, he could almost hear his thoughts forming.

The only thing that broke the sound of the crashing waves was the occasional cry of a passing seagull.

Here and there, he saw the gulls spreading their wings as they hurried to desert the beach, flying inland to seek shelter.

There was a storm coming.

How about that, the weatherman might actually be right for a change, Trevor mused.

He vaguely recalled hearing a prediction of rain hitting the coast by tomorrow. He'd believe it when he saw it. Granted, this could be regarded as the beginning of the region's rainy season, but the last few years had come and gone with less rain than was needed to sustain an aquarium. Southern California was all but bone-dry. It would have taken very little to officially declare a drought.

At this point, the so-called rainy season was going

the way of the unicorn and the dragon, myths for the very young.

Sunshine was good for business, Trevor thought, but not for the land. When it rained, people tended to stay in their homes, or call for takeout rather than drive down to the beach to dine in a restaurant. Still, Trevor wished it would rain, at least for a little while. Parched brown was far from his favorite color.

Continuing to stare off into the horizon, his eyes narrowed. Was that some kind of a vessel silhouetted against the sky?

He squinted. He could have sworn he saw something large and white in the water.

A yacht?

Or was that just his imagination? Not that he possessed much of one outside the boundaries of his kitchen. But stress could be making him see things that weren't there.

"Get to bed, Trev, you've got a long day ahead of you tomorrow, remember?" he muttered. "Don't go conjuring up things that aren't there." No one in their right mind would be sailing this time of night with a storm brewing. It had to be a trick of the light.

But even so, Trevor dawdled a minute longer, digging his bare feet into the sand, his shoes dangling from his fingertips. He supposed it was silly, but walking barefoot in the sand always made him feel like a kid again.

A kid with a hell of a lot of blessings to count, he reminded himself.

So why, with his life obviously so full, so busy that he didn't have the time to draw in an unscheduled breath, with everything he ever wanted coming true, did he still feel as if something was missing from his life? As if there was supposed to be more, but wasn't?

"Never satisfied, that's your problem," he murmured under his breath.

He had no doubt that that would have been Travis's assessment of the situation if he'd said anything to his brother. Travis was one of the two people with whom he shared not only his blood but also his face. He, Travis and Trent were born only minutes apart. Triplets so identical that for the first few years, not even his parents or his older brother, Mike, could tell them apart if not for a few identifying tricks his father had employed. He'd heard that his father had actually written their names on the soles of their left feet with a laundry marker until his mother had vetoed that practice.

When they got older, he, Trent and Travis had taken full advantage of their communal looks, playing each other for the sole purpose of messing with everyone else's minds.

The sight of triplets tended to do that to people, he thought with a nostalgic smile. It reduced the public at large to confused masses. Entertained, he and his brothers had made the most of their situation—until their mother died in a plane crash and their world caved in.

He didn't want to think about that now.

Trevor shoved his free hand deep into his pocket. He didn't want to think about anything, really, just make his mind a blank and recharge, that was the purpose behind this little Lawrence of Arabia trek across the cooling sand.

The boardwalk, newly refurbished and running parallel to the sidewalk some fifty feet away, was right behind him. The car he'd driven to come down here this morning wasn't much beyond that, in the restaurant's parking lot. Trevor began to turn toward it, thinking that he needed to put his shoes back on and get home already, when something caught his eye.

It was a great deal closer than the vessel, which got smaller by the moment, off to whatever destination it had charted.

Closer and a lot less imposing.

He didn't know if it was the moon highlighting it—whatever "it" was—or if some stray beam of light had caught on an object bobbing out in the waves.

No, there was definitely something floating out there.

Probably driftwood or a giant hunk of seaweed, Trevor mocked himself.

Or a shark.

As a kid, he'd been terrified of the movie *Jaws* and all its sequels. So much so that even taking showers required preparatory silent pep talks on his part. For a whole year, he'd taken showers that lasted less than five minutes. His father had praised him for his efforts on behalf of conservation, but Kate knew the real cause. He'd been afraid that the water would attract the finny predator. Without saying anything to him directly, she'd made a point of taking him and his brothers on a field trip to the Aquarium of the Pacific in Long Beach as well as Sea World. Eventually, his phobia faded.

Whatever was out there kept splashing.

Sharks didn't splash like that, he thought. What if it was a person?

What the hell would a person be doing in the middle of the water at this time of night? It didn't make any sense.

But sense or not, his gut told him he was right. Someone was out there. Someone in trouble.

Before he even completed the thought, Trevor found himself running to the edge of the water. He dropped his shoes and shrugged out of his jacket as he made his way into the waves.

"Hey!" he shouted as loud as he could. "You need help out there?" It was a stupid question, but he wanted the person in the water to know that they weren't alone. That help was coming.

There was no answer, only the sound of the waves reaching the shore. That, and another piercing announcement from a seagull.

The closer Trevor got to the edge of the water, the more convinced he was that a human being was out there.

He didn't hesitate.

Trevor dove into the water, fighting to keep his orientation foremost in his mind. He could easily lose his bearings out here in the water, especially in the dark. The water was warmer than he'd expected. Also rougher, but he was a strong swimmer, thanks to the lessons he and his brothers had taken. He could remember not wanting to, but Kate had insisted, saying he never knew when it might come in handy.

How right she was.

Trevor struggled to keep his mouth closed as a wave washed over him, trying to pull him down. His shoulders protested against the effort. He couldn't remember the last time he'd been swimming. His life left no room for things like that. He'd spent the last two years getting his restaurant on its feet and the five years before that either in college or the culinary academy.

He was the one they'd made the nursery rhyme about, the one bemoaning Jack being all work and no play. The closest he'd come to "play" was when he got together with his parents, and his brothers and sister. They insisted he kick back, and he did, as much as he was able. But in his head, he was always working, always planning the next menu, the next banquet. He'd been hired for a number of those and his reputation, mercifully, was spreading by word of mouth.

"Almost there!" he called out, trying not to gasp the words.

And then, bobbing up and down in the swirling dark waters, he'd reached the person.

It was a woman.

The moment he was close to her, he saw her eyelashes flutter and then her eyes roll upward. Damn it, she was passing out. Was she hurt? How did she get here in the first place? Had she fallen off the yacht he'd thought he'd seen a few minutes ago?

Dozens of questions flew in and out of his brain like a bolt of lightning, yielding no answers. He grabbed at her before she could sink.

Maybe it was better this way. If she was unconscious, at least she wouldn't be flailing wildly with her arms or clutching at him to help keep her afloat. Either way she would have been a liability, endangering them both.

Trevor looked toward the shore. God, but it seemed like a long distance away. Turning the unconscious woman so that she was floating on her back, he tucked one arm around her waist as best he could and used the other to swim.

It was awkward at best and progress was slow. The waves seemed to be against him, pushing him back by half the distance he'd made.

It felt like an ongoing battle, one he couldn't even begin to think about losing. No one knew he was out here. His family wouldn't know what to think if all trace of him disappeared into the ocean.

He couldn't do that to them.

Exhausted, he willed strength into his body, focusing on the shore and nothing else. He *had* to reach it. Nothing else was an option.

It seemed as if it was taking forever.

His lungs were burning and his quadriceps felt as if they were on fire. He pressed on, tightening his hold on the woman.

By the time he finally reached the shore, his heart was racing, his head throbbing. He felt as if he'd swallowed a third of the ocean. Dragging her out and collapsing, he just lay there beside the woman he'd rescued, gasping for air, searching for precious equilibrium.

As his breathing returned to a normal rhythm, he realized that the woman beside him wasn't making any noise. She wasn't gasping, wasn't wheezing or coughing.

Wasn't breathing at all.

Turning his head toward her, he noticed that her

chest wasn't rising and falling. She was as still as a dress-shop mannequin.

"Damn it!"

Scrambling to his knees, his own head spinning, Trevor struggled to remain upright as he began CPR. Again, he silently blessed Kate for her foresight because she had been the one to insist that they all— herself included—enroll in a class that taught CPR because "You never know when that kind of thing might come in handy."

She'd gone on to tease that if any of their pranks— far more subdued now that she was in their lives— would cause her heart to stop, they would at least know what to do.

It wasn't working. The woman wasn't coming around, wasn't breathing.

"C'mon, lady, I didn't almost drown trying to save you just to have you die on me out here. Breathe, damn it, breathe!"

Rather than give up, Trevor went at the compressions more forcefully. Breathing into her tilted mouth proved to be harder, because he had very little air to spare, but he doggedly continued, doing what he could, refusing to give up.

She was going to breathe and that's all there was to it.

He wasn't sure just how long he was there, pressing her chest and then blowing air into her mouth. "Forever" echoed in his mind.

Just as his endurance splintered, the woman opened

her eyes. The moment she did, a startled, wary look came into them.

Reflecting back later, Trevor realized he should have guessed she'd be confused and scared. The woman had opened her eyes to find a man pressing his hands against her chest, his mouth hovering above hers, still damp with the imprint of her lips.

Coughing and spurting, the woman bolted upright, pushing him away. She scrambled back from him at the same time as her feet struggled for some kind of traction against the sand.

"What the hell do you think you're doing?" she demanded hoarsely, her eyes wide with anger.

"Saving your life," he told her simply. Still on his knees, Trevor bent over farther, pushing her dark red hair away from her face.

Incensed, afraid and completely disoriented, she slapped away his hand. "Looks more like you're trying to maul me," she accused.

Okay, he'd almost just drowned here, trying to save this woman's life. He didn't expect a ticker-tape parade, but a little civility would have been nice.

"Right," he said, exhaling the word in exasperation. "I come out here every night, trolling for bodies riding on the waves, looking to cop a feel." He rose to his feet, glaring at her. "You were drowning, lady. In case it escaped you, I just saved your life." His voice grew colder, more sarcastic. "In lieu of a sizable donation to my favorite charity, a simple 'thank you' will suffice."

She frowned as she tried to get up to her feet. Her

frown deepened when Trevor offered her his hand. She wanted to ignore it, but even she had to admit she was too wobbly to make it up on her own. Muttering, "Don't try anything else," she took the hand he extended.

But once on her feet, she began to sway again. Trevor caught her before she fell, automatically pulling her against him.

A displeased cry died on her lips as her eyes rolled back in her head for a second time.

She was unconscious again.

Trevor sighed and shook his head. "Second verse, same as the first."

Picking her up into his arms, he walked toward the nearest wooden bench and laid the woman down as gently as possible. He began to rub her wrists and arms, trying to get a little circulation going.

Her dress was plastered to her body. Wet, it looked almost see-through. It obviously offered her very little protection against the escalating wind. It also left very little to his imagination.

She had one hell of a body.

Trevor left her for a moment, hurrying off to where he'd dropped his jacket and shoes. He picked up both, then returned and covered her with his jacket. He checked the cell phone that had been in his pants pocket for the duration of his deep-sea adventure. Soggy, it had died. There was no calling for help.

He began rubbing her arms again. It was several minutes before she opened her eyes for a second time. Trevor braced himself for another waspish confrontation, but this time, she seemed too weak. Instead, she put her hand to her head, as if it was hurting. Squinting at him, he heard her say, "Name?"

"Trevor Marlowe," he told her. "I—"

"No—" impatience echoed in her frustrated, hoarse whisper "—mine."

Chapter Two

Trevor sat back on his heels, eyeing the woman he'd just rescued. She couldn't mean what he thought she meant.

"What do you mean 'mine?'"

She struggled to sit up. This time, he gently but forcefully held her down. Anger flickered in her eyes, but he didn't back away. His hands remained on her shoulders, pinning her down. There was no way she could move. She had no choice but to submit. It didn't make her happy.

"I mean what's my name?" she retorted.

Trevor quickly scanned her forehead, looking for a sign that she'd sustained a blow. But there was no gash, no telltale fresh abrasions or bump to indicate the possible cause of this dearth of information.

"You don't know your name?" He looked at her skeptically.

The level of exasperation rose in her voice. What was he, an idiot? "I wouldn't be asking you if I did."

Trevor still wasn't buying into this a hundred percent. Maybe she just had a macabre sense of humor. "This isn't a joke?"

Fighting a wave of uneasy fear, the redhead spat out, "Do I look like I'm joking?"

"I have no idea," he told her honestly. "I don't know you."

Fear mushroomed within her. There was something about lying here, horizontal, under this man's intense perusal that stripped her of her strength, not to mention her capacity to think. She grabbed the side of the bench and pulled herself upright.

He'd said something that offered her a glimmer of hope in the appalling darkness. At least he'd cleared up one thing for her.

"So, my not remembering you, that's okay?" She saw his brows draw together. She knew she wasn't being very clear, but everything was still hopelessly jumbled in her head, like puzzle pieces thrown haphazardly out of a box. "I mean, I don't know you, right?"

Trevor shook his head. He would have remembered if a woman the likes of this one had passed his line of vision. "No, not from Adam."

"Adam?"

She thought he meant an actual person, Trevor realized. It would have been funny—if the situation weren't so real. "It's just an expression. Never mind." He blew out a frustrated breath, thinking. "What's the last thing that you remember?"

She closed her eyes, as if that could help her focus. By the expression on her face when she opened them again, it hadn't.

"Water."

"Okay," he said gamely. Obviously this was going to require a bit of patience on his part. "Before that."

The woman took a deep breath. He watched her eyes. In the light from the streetlamp just to the right of the bench, they looked to be a deep, intense green. And troubled. Very troubled.

"Nothing," she answered.

He saw that her eyes glistened. Oh, God, not tears. He had no idea what to do with tears. Ordinarily, he'd pretend they weren't there, but he was looking at her face dead-on. If those tears took shape and started to fall, no way could he act as if he didn't see them.

He hadn't a clue what to say.

"I don't remember *anything*," the woman told him. He heard the fear mounting in her voice.

She was really trying not to panic. Trevor could all but see the struggle going on within her. She clenched her hands into fists on either side of her body.

"No, that's not true," he contradicted in a calm, soothing voice.

But his words only seemed to fan the fires already threatening to go out of control.

"Look, you're not inside this head—I am and there's

nothing. Not a damn thing." She pressed her lips together to keep a wave of hysteria from bursting out.

Trevor went on as if she hadn't said a word. "You remember how to talk. You speak English without an accent, international or regional, so most likely, you're a native Californian, most likely from around here."

"Terrific, that makes me one of what, forty million people?"

"You remembered that," he pointed out. "Things are coming back to you, just waiting to be plucked out of the air." Before she could utter another sarcastic contradiction, Trevor instructed, "Close your eyes again and think."

"About what?" she demanded. "I don't remember anything—except how many people there are in Southern California," she qualified angrily before he could mention that extraneous bit of information again.

Trevor took the display of temper in stride. "I think we can safely rule out that you're an anger-management counselor. Humor me," he told her. "Close your eyes and see if anything comes to you." Obviously annoyed, the woman did as she was told. "Anything?" he asked after she said nothing for several seconds.

"Yeah." She opened her eyes. "I'm hungry. And cold."

That wasn't what he was hoping to hear. "Anything else?"

She pressed her lips together. "And I need to go to the bathroom."

He would have laughed then if he didn't feel almost as frustrated as she did. "There's one right there," he said, pointing to the public bathroom.

The bathroom was located less than fifty feet away from their bench. Directly in front of the square, stucco building were two outdoor showers, there specifically for people to wash the salt water off their bodies before going back into their cars. Occasionally, in the dead of summer nights, the showers were used by homeless people who longed to feel clean again.

As the woman got up, so did Trevor. There was un-abashed suspicion in her eyes as she stopped walking and glared at him.

"You're not going in with me, are you?"

"Wasn't planning to," he answered mildly. "Just want to make sure you're steady on your feet. You already passed out once," he reminded her. By the way she frowned, he surmised that somewhere within her now blank world was a woman who liked her independence. Possibly more than the average female, he judged.

"And then what?" she asked as she crossed over to the short, squat building. To her horror, there was no outer door.

"Excuse me?"

She turned around, blocking the building's entrance. "After you walk me to the bathroom, then what?" She appeared uneasy as she asked, "Are you going home?"

That had been the plan, to go home and recharge for tomorrow. But now things had grown complicated. He couldn't just abandon her, yet who was she to him? And she obviously resented his being around her. So, instead of answering her directly, he answered, "You said you were hungry."

"Yes," she admitted warily.

Trevor couldn't help wondering if she as always this suspicious, or if her present situation had transformed her. "I'll take you to Kate's Kitchen and get you something to eat."

"Kate's Kitchen," she repeated. The words meant nothing to her. "Is that like a homeless shelter, or someone's house?"

"Neither. That's my restaurant."

Even within the context of this minor conversation, mentioning his restaurant filled him with pride. It always did. Having it, running it, had been his goal for a very long time.

She made what seemed to her a logical assumption. "You work in a restaurant?"

Trevor corrected her. "I own a restaurant."

"Oh." The single-syllable word was pregnant with meaning and respect—and she hadn't a clue as to why.

Did she own anything? she wondered. It infuriated her that she didn't know. This was going on too long, she silently raged. It was as if she were standing in front of a huge, white wall that was locking her out of everything. She couldn't find the door, couldn't find any way to enter. The worst was that she didn't even know what was behind the wall, if anything.

Standing before the entrance to the public bathroom, she hesitated for a moment. She hated this vulnerable feeling. Hated giving in to it or even acknowledging its existence.

But a survival instinct told her that it was necessary. She turned to glance over her shoulder at the man who'd rescued her. The man she probably owed her life to. "You'll be here when I come out?"

He nodded and she thought she saw a hint of a smile on his lips. Probably laughing at her, she thought. But she had no choice. She couldn't just wander around on the beach at this time of night.

"I'll be here," he promised her.

She had no idea why, but she believed him.

Still, she hurried inside the building to one of the three stalls. None of the doors met and the floor was cold, with sand clinging to the stone here and there, rubbing off on her feet. Shivering as she entered the stall farthest from the doorway, she realized that she didn't have any shoes on.

Had she lost them in the ocean? Or before?

Nothing came to her.

Within less than a minute, she was finished and standing before the sink closest to the door. She looked at her reflection in the badly cracked mirror. She didn't recognize the woman with the plastered, chin-length red hair.

Oh, God, who was she? Was someone out there searching for her?

She looked down at her left hand. There was no ring, but she did notice a tan line encircling it. *Had* there been a ring there? Had she been mugged for that ring? Left for dead? Tossed overboard?

What? her mind screamed.

No answers came in response.

Blowing out a breath, she turned on the faucet. A rumbling noise preceded the emergence of lukewarm water. At least it was clear and not rust-colored. Cupping her hands together, she caught some and threw it on her face, wishing desperately that the simple action would be enough to make her remember.

It wasn't.

"You okay in there?"

She jumped when she heard the man—Trevor, was it?—call out the question. Her heart hammered.

"Just peachy," she heard herself respond.

Even to her own ears, it didn't sound right. There was an angry edge in her voice, which shamed her. This guy, this restaurant owner, didn't have to help her. Didn't have to risk his life to rescue her from a watery grave. Why was she being so nasty to him?

"Sorry," she called out. "I don't mean to be taking this out on you. I just want to remember. I *should* remember," she insisted.

Because she'd tendered a half apology, Trevor's annoyance with her instantly abated. It took very little to get on his good side.

"You're going through a lot," he told her soothingly. She came out then, the expression on her flawless face just a shade contrite. It was all he needed. "C'mon," he urged, "I'll take you to the restaurant. It's within walking distance."

Rather than guide her toward the parking lot, he indicated that they were going to go in the opposite direction.

As he placed his hand to the small of her back, he felt her stiffen beneath his fingertips. Giving no indication that he'd noticed, he dropped his hand to his side.

"The restaurant's right over here."

She stopped and looked at the blue-and-gray stucco

single-story building. Navy-blue trim outlined the door and windows. The building went on for half a city block. A terrace ran along the length of the back of the restaurant. The tables and chairs that usually occupied it during working hours were tucked just inside a wall of glass for the night.

It looked nice. Inviting, even in the darkness. "This is yours?"

Taking his key out, he unlocked the door and then held it open for her. "Mine and the bank's."

She walked in front of him. He hit a switch to the right of the door. Lights came on, illuminating the way.

It was homey, she thought, as she scanned the interior. Warm. She liked it.

"It's nice," she commented. Desperate to find something familiar to grasp, she continued her search over to the reception desk. Nothing around her nudged at any distant images. Still, she heard herself asking, "Have I ever been in here before?"

He turned on another series of lights, not wanting her to feel any more disoriented. "Not that I know of, but then, I'm usually in the kitchen." He only came out on occasion, when someone he knew was in the dining area.

When he said he owned the restaurant, she'd thought of the financial end. She hadn't thought of him in any other capacity. Cocking her head, she tried to picture him at a stove, surrounded with boiling pots.

"You're a chef?"

Trevor smiled, thinking of the diploma from the culinary academy that hung on the wall of his tiny office in the back. "So I like to think."

"Who's Kate?" she asked suddenly, turning toward him. "Your wife?"

"My stepmother."

"Oh." Now that was odd. Most people thought of step-mothers as creatures to get away from, not immortalize. She had no idea where the thought came from, but it took root, planting itself firmly in her mind. Did she have a stepmother? Was that why she felt like that?

"That's a little strange." And then she realized that she'd said the words out loud. She didn't want to offend him, not after he'd rescued her. "Sorry, none of my business."

He couldn't help wondering what sort of unsavory scenario she'd just conjured up in her mind. Something from her past? Was she remembering?

"My stepmother came to work for my dad as our nanny a little more than twenty years ago. She basically saved our lives—not the way I saved yours," he qualified, "but in a sense, just as dramatically." On the outside, they had seemed like a family, but inside, they'd all kept to themselves, at least as far as the pain was concerned. Losing their mother had been hard on all of them. "She brought a lot of happiness into our world and she's been supportive of all of us from the first day, even when we gave her a hard time."

Trevor continued turning on lights as he went toward the rear of the restaurant, to where the walk-in refrigera-tor was located.

She followed him, but she'd stopped listening right after Trevor had said the part about saving her life. It came home to her in letters ten feet high.

He had saved her life.

If not for this man, she would have quite possibly died in that ocean.

By design?

By accident?

Damn it, why wasn't anything coming back to her? she silently demanded. Why didn't she even know her own name? At least the first name, if not the last.

Lost in thought, she impotently clenched her hands into fists again and sighed, struggling to keep her frustration in check.

He heard the loud sigh. Trevor doubted the woman was even aware of it. Opening the door to the refrigerator, he took a step in, then looked around at several racks containing covered pans.

"Can you remember liking anything in particular?" he asked her. When there was no answer, he turned to glance at her over his shoulder. There was a puzzled expression on her face. "Food," he specified. "Can you remember a favorite food?" She seemed to be trying to remember, but then shook her head. "Okay then," he said philosophically. "Maybe this'll be your new favorite food."

He took out a tray, placed a serving on a subdued Wedgwood blue plate and stuck it into the microwave. A minute and a half later, he took out a warm plate of chicken tetrazzini. It had been on this evening's menu. While it was always a popular item, he'd had a few servings left when he closed his doors.

Tomorrow, everything that hadn't been consumed today would find its way to St. Anne's Homeless Shelter.

Luther, a man who had worked and lived at the shelter these last twelve years, came by every morning at eight to pick up the leftovers. Trevor made sure that there always were some, even if he had to prepare them that morning. Luther never left empty-handed.

But this serving was for his mermaid, he thought, bringing it over to the table where, during business hours, the salads were prepared.

She stood on ceremony for exactly half a minute, then ate with gusto.

He liked seeing people enjoy his food like this, although, to be fair, the woman would have probably enjoyed anything at this point. She seemed to be as ravenous as she'd claimed.

The entire serving was gone within less than ten minutes. He supposed that nearly drowning spiked a person's appetite.

"More?" he asked when she pushed the empty plate away from her.

Smiling for the first time since he'd saved her, the woman shook her head. She had a nice smile, Trevor thought.

"No, I'm full." She resisted the urge to run her fingers over the plate and lick them. "And it was very good. You made this?"

It was one of the first things he'd ever learned to prepare. He'd been seven and Kate had made him her assistant, tying one of her aprons around his waist. It had dragged on the floor, but he'd had the time of his life. He'd gotten hooked on cooking from the very start.

"It's an old stand-by," he answered.

"Well, it's very good," she repeated, her tone sounding a little awkward. "Thank you."

He saw concern slip over her face. "What?"

She tried not to let the anxiety take her prisoner. "That's it exactly. 'What?' What do I do now?"

"Well, if you want my opinion," he said, "I think you should be checked out at a hospital. Just in case."

She frowned. At the mention of the word *hospital,* she felt something tighten inside. Was she afraid of hospitals? Had she had a bad experience? Had someone she cared about died in a hospital? It was so terribly annoying, not having a single answer, a single clue to anything about herself.

"I'm okay," she answered.

"You have amnesia," Trevor pointed out to her. "That's not okay."

She followed him out into the dining hall again. "But they can't fix that in a hospital, can they?"

"I don't know, but this way, you find out if you have a concussion, or anything else wrong." Although from where he sat, she looked damn near perfect, at least on the outside, he mused.

He kept the thought to himself.

"They're going to want to know my name," she said.

"We'll just tell them that you can't remember it."

We. Did that mean he was coming with her? She had no idea why, but the thought brought her a sense of relief.

"But I need a name," she protested. She raised her eyes to his, silently asking him to christen her, if only for the time being.

"Okay." Fishing out his keys, he thought for a moment. "How about 'Venus'?"

"Venus?" she echoed. It was pretty. She liked it.

He nodded as he locked the door behind them and then armed the security system. "Like the Botticelli painting. Venus rising out of the sea—"

"On a giant half shell," she completed.

Her eyes widened.

Chapter Three

"I remember that," she cried excitedly.

Without thinking, she grabbed at his shirtfront. The jacket he'd put around her began to slip off, but he caught it in time and set it back on her shoulders. She was vaguely aware of an electrical charge dancing through her, but her excitement was focused on this tiny kernel of information that she'd stumbled across.

She searched his face for an answer. "How do I remember that?"

Very gently, he disengaged her hands from his shirt. "You're an artist, you work in the art field, or maybe you just like Botticelli. Or clams," he added, picking up on her description of the half shell. "Or maybe your memory's coming back. Can you remember anything else?" he prodded.

Like a child trying to recall a phrase she'd memorized, the woman slid her tongue along her lips, a faraway look in her eyes. Trevor watched her and could almost see her effort to summon a familiar thought, *any* familiar thought.

Her frustration was apparent when she shook her head.

"No." She exhaled the words. "Nothing else."

Pocketing his keys, he began walking. She fell into step. "Maybe you shouldn't try so hard, then," he suggested. "It'll come back on its own. Like the Botticelli painting."

She dragged her hand through her hair. Disappointment was evident in every word. "Not fast enough for me."

He resisted the temptation to put his arm around her shoulders, sensing that the gesture wouldn't be welcomed. "C'mon, Venus, let's get you checked out."

Stumbling blocks became evident. "I don't have any money," she told him even as she followed him to the far side of the restaurant's perimeter, where the parking lot was located.

One lone car stood unattended. His, she surmised. He drove a Mustang. While she recognized the vehicle's make and model, it meant nothing to her. No bells rang, no fragments of memory were dislodged. It was annoying beyond words.

She stopped before the car, waiting for him to unlock it. "And since I don't know who I am, I don't have any medical insurance." She saw him look up at her. He seemed a great deal happier than she did. "Why are you grinning like that?"

Aiming his key at the car, he pressed a button and disarmed the vehicle's security system. All four locks sprang to attention. "You just remembered that you need medical insurance."

She paused for a second before getting into the Mustang. She felt a great deal less pleased about this supposed breakthrough. "You're right, I did. But if I can remember something that trivial, why can't I remember who the hell I am?"

Opening his car door, Trevor got in. She followed suit on her side. "Maybe you don't want to."

She frowned. "That's ridiculous. Why wouldn't I want to remember who I am?"

Psychology wasn't his thing—that belonged to Kate and his brother Trent. But he'd heard enough about the topic at home to venture an educated guess. "Maybe you're running from something. Something that involves who you are."

Her frown deepened. "That's a little far-fetched, isn't it?"

Inserting the key into the ignition, Trevor shrugged. "Just a thought." He glanced at her. "You remembered to buckle up."

Her irritation increased. Did he think she was a child in need of endless encouragement? "All right, I get it. I remember some things. Some *general* things," she emphasized. It was in the same category as remembering how to walk and talk. "You don't have to keep pointing those things out."

He started up the car. "Just trying to give you some hope, Venus."

Guilt assaulted her. She was being waspish again—and he was being nice and definitely going out of his way for her. He didn't have to be doing any of this. "Are you sure I don't know you?"

Leaving the lot, he made a left turn, easing onto Pacific Coast Highway. The hospital, Blair Memorial, wasn't far. "I'm sure."

It didn't make any sense to her. Something told her that she was accustomed to people who didn't go out of their way for anyone. The thought made her sad. "If you don't know me, then why are you going out of your way like this?"

"Can't very well save your life then just say, 'See ya,' and go on my way, now can I?"

Why couldn't he? she wondered. "Wouldn't most people?"

"I don't know people like that." Coming to a red light, he eased onto the brake and spared her a look. "But you obviously do."

She became defensive without knowing why. "How do you know that?"

"Because you wouldn't have asked that question if you didn't," he told her simply. "It wouldn't have been in your 'general' frame of reference." He emphasized the word she'd balked at previously.

She thought about it for a minute. Without knowing it, he'd hit upon the same thought she'd had, except that hers involved an uneasy feeling. "That's pretty good. You always this logical?"

Being creative, he'd never thought about being logical.

But he did now. He realized logic pretty much dictated a good portion of his life. Unlike Travis, he didn't act first then think later. He did it the other way around—except when it had come to rescuing Venus. He'd reacted rather than reasoned. But, looking back, he supposed logic came into play even there. Because if he'd stood by and done nothing, her life—and death—would have weighed heavily on his conscience.

But he didn't want to get into a discussion about himself. It was her they needed to identify, not him.

"Mostly," he admitted.

She nodded her head. She appeared complacent, but then she challenged him. This was a woman to keep you on your toes, he noted.

"Then tell me how you can logically take me to a hospital to be checked out when I have no money and no identity?" she asked. "They're going to want to get paid."

"Don't worry about that." He could feel her eyes on him. The woman obviously wanted details. He deliberately remained vague, not wanting to get into an argument. She was already displaying more than the average share of pride. "I'll take care of it."

Which meant he was going to pay for her care out of his own pocket—unless he owned a hospital as well as a restaurant.

"If I'm a stranger to you, why would you do that?" she asked.

Because he'd been raised to lend a helping hand when he could. But he had feeling if he told her that, it would sound too much like charity. "In some cultures, if you save a life, it's yours. That means you have to take care of it."

Venus shook her head. "This isn't one of those cultures."

"Something else you know," he said cheerfully. He had no idea why he was enjoying himself so much, but he was. "You can pay me back when your memory returns," he told her. He slanted a look in her direction, then turned back to the road. "That satisfy you?"

"I guess it'll have to."

She thought for a moment, then examined at his profile, wondering if she'd just had some kind of a breakthrough. The rest of her mind still felt tangled. But right now, a few fragments floated through her brain. Fragments that seemed familiar, even though she couldn't harness them. It was all too vague. And so damn aggravating.

She sighed, giving voice to her discovery. "I don't think I like being beholden to anyone."

"Nothing wrong in asking for help once in a while."

"There is if asking for help places you in someone's debt."

There was a long stretch between lights. He took advantage of it by stepping on the gas, careful to remain on the alert for the occasional motorcycle cop. "That sounds as if you've had some not overly satisfactory relationships with people."

He was right. It did sound that way. Was this another piece of the puzzle that contained her identity? Venus tried vainly to fit it in somewhere. She struck out.

"I don't know," she admitted. But even as she said the words, something nebulous slipped over her. It was elusive and refused to take on any definite form, but came with a feeling that there was some truth in what he said.

He hadn't expected her to suddenly exclaim, "Eureka!" and have her memory rush back. But he had no doubt that eventually, the woman would remember things. Just not yet.

"Maybe you were just born skeptical," he theorized.

"Maybe," she mumbled under her breath. She might not have been born that way, but she felt it now.

Pacific Coast Highway and Newport Boulevard were fairly empty at this time of night. Trevor made the trip from Kate's Kitchen to Blair Memorial in record time.

Luck continued to hold for them because, judging by the hospital's emergency room parking lot, it had been a rather slow night at Blair, as well. Two minutes after they entered through the electronic doors, Venus was sitting down in a chair before the receptionist. Rather than take the chair next to her, he stood behind her.

The woman on the other side of the desk had to be approaching retirement age and was definitely cheerful. She gave each of them a wide smile as they approached her.

"You caught us at a good time," the receptionist, Rebecca according to the name tag pinned to her left shoulder, told them. "So, what brings you to the emergency room tonight?"

"He did," Venus answered, turning her head toward the man behind her.

"She means besides that," Trevor interjected, then took over the narrative. "She almost drowned tonight."

Sympathy flared in the woman's brown eyes as she appraised the would-be patient in front of her. "And you want us to check you out for any ill effects?"

Again, when Venus didn't answer quickly enough, Trevor took over. "The ill effect is that she can't remember who she is or anything about how she got into the ocean to begin with."

"The ocean," the receptionist repeated, looking surprised by the information. And then she nodded. "That would explain the damp clothes," she surmised. The smile on her lips indicated she was a tad chagrined. "I thought you were talking about falling into a swimming pool." Typing, she made a notation on the screen, then automatically asked, "Do you have any identification?"

Impatience had woven through her the second she'd walked through the doors.

"If I did, I'd know who I was, wouldn't I?" Out of the corner of her eye, she saw Trevor flash her a look. Everyone couldn't be as nice as he was, she thought defensively. And she had a feeling that she wasn't in Trevor's league when it came to being laid-back.

"Right." Rebecca hit several keystrokes, then glanced up again. "No insurance cards, either, I take it."

"No anything," Venus replied, doing her best not to sound impatient.

Trevor saw the receptionist look at Venus, then raise her eyes to his. "And how would you like to—"

Trevor anticipated her. Before the receptionist could find a comfortable way to ask the question, he had his wallet out and produced a credit card. Leaning over the desk, he handed it to her.

"Put it on my card," he instructed.

After taking the card from him, the receptionist rose. "I'll be right back," she promised. "I just have to run this through."

"I don't feel comfortable about this," Venus told him as the receptionist went to a room behind the registration area.

"It shouldn't take too long," he assured her. In his opinion, she really needed to get checked out, just in case something was wrong. "She said they weren't busy tonight."

Venus waved away his words. "No, I mean having you put this on your credit card." It was hard to believe selfless people like this man were still around. "How do you know I won't skip out on you once my memory comes back?" she challenged.

"I just know." When she looked at him skeptically, he added, "Call it a hunch."

"I call it being foolhardy," she retorted.

"Why?" His mouth curved in amusement. "*Are* you planning on skipping out once your memory returns?"

"No," she answered with feeling. "But you don't know that for sure."

He gazed into her eyes and her stomach went queasy. That was twice now that she'd reacted to him this way. Why?

"I just know," he told her softly.

The receptionist returned with the paperwork before Venus had a chance to challenge Trevor again. He signed on the line allotted for his signature. In less time than it took to house the paperwork in a folder, they were being ushered into the rear of the emergency room where all the beds were.

Most of them were empty.

The attending nurse took down more information, although it, too, was sparse beyond Trevor's recounting of the events. Venus had nothing to add because she couldn't remember.

X-rays and blood work were ordered.

An orderly wheeled her away to the lab, leaving Trevor to sit and wait and wonder if he was getting in over his head. Normally, these days, the most interaction he had with women outside his family was to ask them if everything was all right with their meal. He couldn't remember the last time he'd been out socially.

The thought made him smile. His father and Kate would be happy about this. Any girl in a storm.

The physician on duty reviewed the films and glanced at the lab report. His expression indicated that he was unimpressed by either.

"Everything looks normal," he declared, returning the X-rays to the oversize manila envelope that protected them.

"But I can't remember anything," Venus protested.

The physician seemed fairly unconcerned. "There's no evidence of a concussion and no tumors or lesions are indicated. Most likely, what you have is a case of hysterical amnesia."

"Hysterical?" she echoed with distaste. Venus didn't

care for the term's connotation. She was fairly certain she wasn't the hysterical type and resented being categorized that way.

"Hysterical amnesia brought on by a trauma, either physical or emotional," the doctor explained. "In either case, most people suffering from that recover their memories in a few days."

Venus zeroed in on the crucial word. "Most people, but not all."

"No, not all," the doctor freely admitted. He glanced at the chart again, then placed it at the foot of her bed. He looked at Trevor as he continued, "But there's no reason to believe that you won't."

"Are there people who never recover from amnesia?"

The emergency room physician appeared reluctant to comment on her question. Venus waited for an answer.

"Every now and again, yes, a few never recover their memory. But again, there's no reason to believe that you'll number among them." A hint of a smile creased his thin lips. "You'll get your memory back."

That wasn't enough. She needed facts. "Give me a good reason to believe that I will."

The doctor seemed weary. It was apparent that he wasn't accustomed to justifying his opinion, but he humored her.

"Well, you're young, healthy and in very good physical condition. Those are the best conditions. Give yourself a little time." He glanced at the man beside her, silently enlisting his aid. "Nearly drowning is a pretty intense experience."

A restlessness continued to consume her. "So's not knowing who you are."

The doctor took a step away from the bed, as if ready to move on. "Well, know this. You're a very lucky young lady that this man was there to save you." He addressed his next words to Trevor. "She needs to come back in two weeks if she isn't herself by then." Taking out his prescription pad, he wrote something down on the top page, then tore it off. He held the page out to Trevor. "These are to deal with the pain should she have any," he added. "Feel better," he said, then walked quickly away.

Leaning over, Venus took the prescription from Trevor. Not a single word of it made any sense. Just like the jumbled mess in her brain. She sighed. "He seems to think you're in charge of me."

Trevor tried to lighten her obvious dour mood. "Maybe he's aware of the custom I told you about earlier. I saved your life, now it's mine to protect and do what I want with."

Folding the prescription, she started to put it in her pocket, only to realize that she had no pockets and no other place to put the folded piece of paper. With another sigh, she held the prescription out to him.

"I guess you get to hang on to this until I can get a purse—which I can't because I have no money, no identity," she realized. Venus bit the inside of her lip to keep from uttering a string of less than flattering words about her dilemma.

"Sit tight," he instructed, "I'll get this filled for you at the hospital pharmacy."

"Wouldn't they be closed?" She looked at a wall clock directly to her right. "It's after midnight."

"The hospital pharmacy is opened twenty-four/seven," he assured her. "My whole family uses this place. Can't get better care than here."

She nodded as she slid off the side of the bed.

He stopped walking away. "What are you doing? I just said—"

"I'm coming with you." There was no room for debate. Her tone was firm. "And then, after we fill that, we can leave. The sooner we get out of here, the better." When she saw him eyeing her quizzically, she told him, "I don't like hospitals. I don't know why I don't, but I don't." And then she hesitated. Nothing about her was written in stone, she thought helplessly. "At least, I'm pretty sure I don't."

Trevor could empathize. If he were in her place, if the family he loved were erased from his mind, he wouldn't know how he would cope. "It'll all clear up soon," he promised.

"I'll hold you to that," she murmured.

Trevor cut off the engine. They were here. At the homeless shelter, the one he donated all his leftovers to. The one Kate volunteered at whenever her schedule permitted and where he, his brothers, sister and parents had spent more than one Thanksgiving working the kitchen.

St. Anne's was clean, had been renovated less than two years ago and the staff consisted of kind, decent people. There was no reason in the world for him to hesitate in bringing Venus here. They'd take good care of her. They were accustomed to helping the lost, though she was just a little more lost than most.

And yet, he did hesitate. Maybe because St. Anne's was a homeless shelter and somehow, that very fact seemed demoralizing. Venus had already been through enough tonight.

"You'll be all right here," he told her, trying to convince himself more than her.

She nodded. "You already said that. Twice." She took a deep breath and placed her hand on the latch inside the car. But as she began to open the passenger door, Trevor suddenly stepped on the accelerator. They were moving away from the curb.

"Hey," she protested, pulling the door shut. "What are you doing?"

"Taking you someplace else" was all he said.

Chapter Four

"Where are you taking me?" she asked, rebuckling her seat belt as he made his way down the block.

Where.

That was a very good question, Trevor thought. One he couldn't answer. Where did he take a woman who had no memory of life that went back more than four hours into the past?

If this was the middle of the day, he would have taken her to the nearest police precinct and had them handle it. But she couldn't sleep in a police station and she'd told him earlier that she was tired.

She had to be even more tired now. The police station could wait until morning, he reasoned. There was plenty of time for her to fill out the paperwork needed to help find out who she was.

But right now, the woman whose life he'd saved was in need of a bed.

His first impulse was to bring her to his parents' house. He could count on Kate not only to take in Venus, but also to make her feel welcome. And his father went along with almost anything Kate wanted because her heart was always in the right place. Though at times contrary, it was a known fact that Bryan Marlowe doted on his wife.

To appear on their doorstep with a stranger in tow at this time of night would have been a total imposition. They were most likely asleep by now. It wouldn't be fair of him to do that to his parents unless he had no other choice.

And he did, Trevor thought. He could always take her to his place.

Trevor slanted a glance at the woman beside him and wondered how she'd react to that. Would she just go along, or would she think that he had an ulterior motive? He wouldn't blame her if she did. These weren't the most innocent of times.

"Where are you taking me?" Venus repeated when he didn't answer her question.

He kept his eyes on the road. "I'm taking you to my place."

Out of the corner of his eye, he saw her toss her head. Curls the color of flame bounced about her head. "I don't think so."

So much for just going along with it. "I'll take the couch," he offered. "You can have the bedroom. It has a lock on the door," he added quickly before she could utter another protest.

"You can pick a lock." She snorted.

"Picking locks isn't a skill I've ever acquired," he said matter-of-factly, still watching the road. The streets were well-illuminated, but the cover of darkness drew out the drunk drivers, promising to hide them well. Until the point of impact. He was always extra alert driving home after closing up.

He heard Venus blow out an impatient breath. "What are my other options?"

He'd had a hunch she'd ask. "I can turn around and go back to the homeless shelter, or I could drop you off at the police station."

"That's it?"

For the time being, Trevor decided to omit mentioning his parents' house. "That's it."

Venus was silent for a moment. He could almost hear her mulling over the pros and cons. "That lock on the bedroom door really work?"

He could tell what went through her mind. Should he be insulted or flattered? He did want her to understand he wasn't the type to take advantage of a woman—ever.

"Venus, we were alone on the beach and alone in the restaurant. If I'd wanted to do anything with you or to you, I'd have already done it. I don't need to take you to my apartment for that. Understood?"

"Understood." Her next question came out of nowhere and took him by surprise. "Then you don't find me attractive?"

Wow, talk about getting thrown a curve. "I didn't say that." He supposed even a woman with amnesia needed to have her self-esteem reinforced. "What I am saying is that whatever appetites I might have I can keep under control. You don't have anything to worry about from me." He eased his foot off the gas, ready to make a U-turn if he had to. There was no one else on the road for now. "Okay, the choice is up to you. Homeless shelter, police precinct or my apartment. Which will it be?"

Venus was silent for a moment, thinking. The man made a compelling argument for trusting him. But she couldn't help wondering if she would regret this. Still, something inside of her trusted him, although she couldn't have said why.

"Your apartment." And then she frowned.

He glanced at her before easing back on the accelerator. She still looked uncomfortable. Why? Did she want to change her mind?

"What?"

Venus shrugged, feeling helpless as she wandered through this murky mental maze. "I'm trying to remember if I know any self-defense disciplines."

Trevor laughed shortly. The woman was not the trusting type. He supposed that was a good thing. In the same situation, he wouldn't want his sister, Kelsey, to be blindly trusting.

"You won't need them," he assured her. And then he smiled. "We're even on this, you know."

Her frowned deepened as she looked at him, puzzled. "What do you mean?"

"For all I know, you could be a ticking time bomb. This might not have registered with you, but I'm opening my place up to a complete stranger who might just be lying to me."

She didn't seem to hear the comment about lying. "A complete stranger who's—" she looked at the clock on the dashboard "—approximately four hours old, give or take, if you go by the length of my memories."

He empathized, knowing how frustrated he would feel in her position. "That'll improve soon."

God, she so wanted to believe him. "You really believe that?"

His expression was a portrait of sincerity. "Yeah, I do."

But she needed more than that. She needed logical reasons. Reasons the doctor in the E.R. really hadn't provided. "Why?"

"Because I'm basically an optimist."

That wasn't what she was hoping to hear. Venus sighed. "Well, I hope you're right, optimist. I really hope you're right."

So do I. But Trevor kept the thought to himself.

Sunflower Creek Apartment Homes was a complex composed of nearly two hundred garden apartments, none standing taller than two stories. Trevor's was one such apartment, on the second floor. It was halfway between the center of the complex where the community pool was located, and the car ports. The upshot was that particular area was fairly quiet.

At one in the morning it was almost eerily so.

Staying close, Venus followed her rescuer up a flight of stone stairs. The paper slippers she'd gotten from the E.R. swished against each step as she crossed them. She still had on his jacket, but the breeze found its way under the skirt of her dress, sliding along her bare legs and making her shiver.

For some reason, the cold reminded her how truly needy she was, at least for the moment.

Unlocking his door, Trevor walked in and turned on the light, then looked over his shoulder.

"C'mon in," he coaxed. He took a guess at the reason for her apparent apprehension. "There's no one else here, Venus."

"Is there usually someone here?"

"Not when I'm not here." About to put his keys down on the counter, Trevor thought better of it. He tucked the keys back into his pocket. Just in case. It was better to be safe than sorry.

And then he thought of something. "Wait here a second," he told Venus as he went to the rear of the apartment and his bedroom.

Venus barely nodded in response. Instead, she stood there, looking around, feeling she had no idea what, wishing at least one thing could come back to her, however small.

But nothing did.

This was awful. She didn't even know if she was a nice person or not. Were there people out searching for her? Or were they just glad that she'd disappeared?

Or, worse, was she alone and no one even knew she was missing?

In the background, she heard a wardrobe door being slid back and forth. Her frown returned. What was that all about?

The thought no sooner formed in her head than Trevor returned to the living room. He held a blue pullover sweater, a pair of jeans and a pair of almost brand-new sneakers.

"These might fit you," he said, laying everything out on the coffee table.

Venus looked at the three items for a long moment. The clothing looked to be her size. Did they belong to his wife? To his girlfriend? And where was the woman who belonged to these clothes?

She raised her eyes to his. "Well, they're too small for you, so I'm guessing this means you're not a cross-dresser. Won't whoever they belong to mind my wearing them?" she asked.

She was being flippant again. He was becoming familiar with the way her mind worked. She was flippant when something made her uncomfortable. Except that right how, he hadn't a clue what that might be.

"I sincerely doubt it, or she wouldn't have forgotten them when she left."

She. It struck Venus that "she" was a very ambiguous pronoun and she was in no mood for more problems or complications. "'She?'"

"Someone I thought I knew," was all he said.

There was no point in going into the single largest disappointment of his life. While they were together, he'd thought Alicia was the one, the woman he was meant to spend the rest of his life with, the way his father was meant to spend the rest of his with Kate. But he'd been too busy trying to lay the foundations down for a future for them. He'd realized too late that they'd not only drifted apart, but she had also gone paddling in a completely different ocean.

He'd come home early one evening, a bottle of champagne in his hand, determined to surprise her. He turned out to be the one who was surprised. He'd found her packing. Someone else was in her life, she told him matter-of-factly, for several months now and it had turned serious. They were getting married. She was leaving him and nothing he could say would make her stay.

Stunned, hurt, he couldn't bring himself to ask Alicia to remain, to try to work out their problems. Asking was tantamount to begging as far as he was concerned and a relationship based on begging wasn't worth having—or saving.

"I'm not sure about the sneakers," he went on as if Venus hadn't asked him anything. "But for now, they're better than nothing. We can see about getting you a better pair of shoes tomorrow."

We. Tomorrow. He was making plans for her, about her. Without asking. Part of her felt protected, the other part felt threatened and trapped.

A quip shot to her lips. She pressed them together, hard, holding back the remark and banking down the urge to deflect any offers of help. She needed help and she knew it. God knew she was in no position to just march off on her own. She had no money, no memory and, without Trevor, no shoes.

Definitely not the mistress of her own fate, she thought, hating the feeling. She supposed, in all fairness, it could be worse.

Mustering the best smile she could, her mouth curved only a little as she murmured, "Thank you."

"Don't mention it. Bedroom's right through there." He pointed it out to her.

Venus picked up the sweater, jeans and sneakers, holding them against her. She started to go, then stopped. Trevor was taking the decorative pillows off the sofa. Aware that she had stopped walking out of the room, he looked at her.

"Something wrong?"

Other than not being able to remember who the hell I am, no, nothing's wrong. Everything is ginger-peachy. "I feel bad, chasing you out of your own bed like this," she confessed.

"You're not," he told her. "I offered you the use of the room, remember?" He nodded again toward the bedroom, indicating that she should leave. "See you in the morning, Venus."

Venus, goddess of love. She didn't feel like a goddess right now. Unless it was that armless one. Venus de Milo, was it? The name sounded right, but she just wasn't sure.

Wasn't sure about *anything*.

"G'night," she murmured, clutching the clothes he'd given her to her chest as she walked out of the living room.

Trevor discovered his couch was not fashioned for comfort as a bed. As a torture rack, it had definite possibilities. He wasn't one of those overwrought creatures whose thoughts and worries kept him awake for half the night. Falling asleep and staying there was not a recurring problem for him.

But sleeping on a rock-hard surface was not a skill that he'd honed. He tossed and turned for most of what was left of the night, then fell asleep some time after four.

The smell of food woke him.

Specifically, the aroma of coffee, deep, rich and inviting, penetrated the perimeters of his ragged rest, breaking down the flimsy walls surrounding him.

That and the scent of freshly made pancakes.

His eyes flew open.

For a moment, disorientation hovered over his brain. By virtue of the aroma, he figured he was home. The home where he had grown up. And Kate was making breakfast for all of them the way she used to.

Blinking, his surroundings came into focus, as did his mind, and his aching back.

He was in his apartment, alone.

No, not alone. He'd brought someone home with him last night.

Someone who was currently in his kitchen? It seemed like the logical assumption, except that he would have bet money that the woman he'd saved from a watery grave didn't know her way around the kitchen.

Showed what he knew.

Sitting up, Trevor slipped his loafers back on his feet. He'd slept in his clothes, fully dressed in order to seem less threatening to his impromptu houseguest. Running his hand through his sandy-colored hair, smoothing it down as best he could, Trevor went into the kitchen.

She was wearing the clothes he'd given her. Wearing them differently than Alicia, he noted. Her figure was curvier. Her back was to him, but he could see that she was doing something on the stove. Something that smelled damn good.

"Morning," he said.

She almost dropped the frying pan. The shriek escaped her lips before she could stop it. She turned to glare at him, one hand gripped around the handle of the frying pan, the other hand splayed across her chest, trying to keep her heart from leaping out.

"Do you always sneak up on people like that?" she demanded.

It seemed useless to point out that he wasn't trying to sneak up on her, that he'd attempted to announce himself as best as possible.

"I do if they're in my kitchen when I wake up," he cracked. He looked around her shoulder to see what she was doing on the stove. The aroma took him back. "What's all this?"

She looked at the stove and the pancakes. "If you can't tell, I must be worse at it than I thought. I wanted to make you breakfast."

The protest that there was no need for her to cook faded in light of something more important. "You remember how to make pancakes?"

"I guess. This amnesia thing is pretty damn selective," she lamented and then pressed her lips together, looking very uncertain. "The trouble is I don't know if I know how to make 'good' pancakes or not," she admitted.

He smiled. "They smell good," he said, trying to encourage her. "I'd say that was half the battle."

She caught her bottom lip between her teeth. Something inside his gut tightened as he watched. "Are you willing to try them?"

"Sure, I'm game," he said, then added, "if you join me."

She tried to gauge his thoughts. "Want to make sure I didn't put any poison in them?" she asked glibly.

"No, I just don't like eating alone when there's someone else in the room." It was the truth. Eating to him was a sharing experience.

"Okay." Venus nodded gamely.

She placed three pancakes on a plate and offered the plate to him. Trevor opened a drawer, taking out two sets of forks and knives. He put them on the table as she slid two pancakes onto a second plate, this time for herself. She sat down at the table opposite him.

"Don't feel you have to be polite," she told Trevor. "Just tell me what you think." Despite her disclaimer, she watched him intently as he took the first bite. He'd barely gotten the morsel into his mouth when she asked, "Well?" with an ill-disguised hopeful note in her voice.

He smiled, nodding his head. The moment he did, he could see relief coming into her eyes. It was important to her to be good at something. He could relate to that.

"Looks like you know how to cook, Venus. And damn well, too."

Beaming, she tried to pretend that the compliment

didn't matter. But he could see that it did. Beneath her blasé, flippant attitude was a vulnerable woman. As he took another bite, he couldn't help wondering what had gone into forming both.

Chapter Five

Trevor had more than an average day ahead of him. He hardly had any time for a cup of coffee, much less time to play detective on his apartment guest's behalf.

Venus, or whatever her real name was, needed someone's full attention to her problem, or at least for long enough to get her on her feet. But with a full, thriving lunch crowd coming in and a golden anniversary banquet to prepare that evening, not to mention the fact that he was still short one salad girl, that person wasn't going to be him.

At least, not today.

And it wouldn't be fair for him to ask Venus to wait until tomorrow. Someone might be looking for her right now. He would be if she belonged in his world and had suddenly gone missing.

Which was why, half an hour after he'd eaten the breakfast she'd prepared, Trevor was on the road, with Venus sitting beside him in the passenger seat. He headed to his parents' house, which was located in the neighboring town just twelve miles away.

"I don't feel right about this," Venus told him as she'd taken her seat. Trevor wove in and out of traffic with the ease of a practicing magician. They were approaching his parents' development. "This is an imposition."

And she was a stranger who meant nothing to them. Or him, she reminded herself.

"You'll have to meet my stepmother to understand," he answered. Trevor made a right and then an immediate left to get into the development. The streets were all short, feeding into one another like pieces of a familiar, beloved puzzle. "But I promise you she won't see this as an imposition. She'll see it as something she was meant to do."

The sarcasm came of its own accord, as if it had a life of its own. "How often does she take amnesiacs under her wing?"

She was being flippant again, Trevor thought, steering the car down an oak-tree-lined block. More than the rest of them, Kate, because of her vocation as well as her nature, was better equipped to handle the situation—and make Venus feel at ease.

"As far as I know, you'd be her first. But the point is, she likes helping people," he assured her. "It's what she does, who she is. That's why she went into child psychology in the first place, to help."

And who was she? Venus couldn't help wondering. What did she do for a living? Was some boss impatiently waiting somewhere for her to come in this morning, or didn't it matter to anyone that she wasn't there?

This not knowing anything about herself was really irritating.

"We're here," Trevor announced as he pulled up before a cheery two-story house, parking beside the mailbox.

In the last twenty years, the house had been through two major renovations as well as a couple of minor ones. During that time, bathrooms and the kitchen had been updated, and a pool and Jacuzzi had been installed in the backyard. But even though the exterior of the house had changed, this was still home, still the place where basically good memories of his childhood resided.

"This is home," he announced, turning off the car engine.

Home.

For just half a heartbeat, something hazy and distant flashed across her mind, bringing with it an image of something large and imposing. Austere. Was that her home? Or just something she'd seen once?

Venus suppressed a sigh. She had no way of knowing, no way of turning the glimmer into something more. And already now, the flash receded, fading without a trace. Leaving her even more exasperated.

Venus did her best to hide her frustration. It was bad enough that Trevor imposed on his parents by bringing her to them like some stray puppy. They certainly didn't need someone who was irritably out of sorts as well.

Opening the door on her side, she swung her legs out,

then hesitated for a moment. "You're sure they won't mind? Absolutely, positively sure?"

Trevor had already made his way around the vehicle and now took hold of her arm, gently coaxing her out of the car. "Absolutely, positively," he echoed.

"Okay."

But it wasn't okay. All of this was almost happening against her will and she couldn't even begin to explain how annoying that really was, not to have a say in anything. Not to know what her say would have been if she'd had the option.

Just then, as she turned from the car, Venus saw the front door of the house open. A young woman with long blond hair, held in semi-abeyance by a hair band, came hurrying out. She balanced a backpack, a purse and several extraneous books, trying not to drop anything. The young woman stopped dead in her tracks when she saw them, surprise and then pleasure washing over her fresh young face.

"Mom," she called out, aiming the words over her shoulder and into the house, "I think it's Trevor. And he's got a girl with him!"

Venus didn't know which sentence sounded stranger, that the blonde was surprised that Trevor had brought a woman with him, or that the blonde didn't seem to know if it was him or not.

She looked at the man beside her. "Isn't that your sister?" she asked. When he nodded, she asked, "Why isn't she sure who you are?"

Trevor smiled as he urged her forward. "Because two

of my brothers look pretty much exactly like me." When he saw the puzzled look intensify, he added, "I'm a triplet."

She rolled this newest piece of information over in her head. "So I guess identity crises are right up your alley."

"I know what you're going through better than most," he allowed.

It hadn't been easy, finding his own way. But then again, it hadn't been as difficult as some might think. He'd known early on what he wanted to do with his life and he'd never felt an overwhelming desire to break away from the family, just to march to the drummer he heard in his head. The only time that had been a problem was when he'd faced disappointing his father, who'd wanted him to become a lawyer, like him.

Before Venus could comment any further, another woman emerged out of the house. This one was a slightly older version of the girl with the backpack. A sense of warmth emanated from her. She crossed to them and they met halfway up the driveway.

"Trevor, what a nice surprise," she declared, kissing his cheek. Her warm smile washed over both of them. She looked at her son's companion. "Hello, I'm Kate Marlowe." She waved a hand at the girl with the backpack. "That's Trevor's sister, Kelsey. And you are…?"

A frustrated sigh preceded her answer. "I haven't the slightest idea."

Joining them, Kelsey looked from the woman next to her brother to Trevor. "What does your girlfriend mean, Trev?"

"Hey, what's all the commotion out here?"

Venus turned toward this newest voice. A tall, dark-haired man in a light gray suit stood on the step before the front door. The eyes that met and held hers were filled with curiosity.

Although Trevor had sandy-blond hair, like his step-mother and his sister, Venus could still see a definite family resemblance between the man and Trevor. This had to be his father. He had a nice family.

The moment she thought that, she felt an odd pang in the pit of her stomach. Why? She had no idea and then, the feeling was gone. Like her memory and her identity, she thought ruefully.

"Trevor brought over his girlfriend," Kelsey announced gleefully to her father.

Trevor glanced at Venus. "Sorry about that," he apologized, then looked toward his family. "She's not my girlfriend."

Kelsey had never had trouble speaking up. As the baby of the family, she was accustomed to being indulged. She was also accustomed to fighting to be heard and taken seriously on occasion. "Then who is she?" she asked.

"That is the million-dollar question," Venus answered before Trevor had a chance.

Kate, Bryan and Kelsey exchanged glances, then looked at Trevor for an explanation.

He turned to Venus. In deference to her, he thought they should take the discussion inside rather than go on talking out here.

"Mom, can we go inside?" he suggested.

"Sorry, where are my manners? Of course." Kate gestured toward the doorway. "Please," she insisted, "just go in." Then Kate looked at her husband and her daughter, kissing each in turn. It was meant as an act of loving dismissal. They each had someplace else to be. "I'll see you two tonight—and don't worry," she promised, "I'll fill you both in."

Bryan eyed his son and the woman Trevor had brought with him as they disappeared into the house. Life with Kate had activated his curiosity gland.

"Call me as soon as you find out what's going on," he instructed.

"Ditto," Kelsey added her voice to the request.

Nodding, Kate smiled. Rather than say yes, she promised, "I'll do my best."

Her intuition told her that this was not exactly a run-of-the-mill situation. That meant that Trevor might ask her not to repeat something. She was very careful not to betray a confidence, even if that meant withholding information from another member of the family. Her word was everything to her—and to them.

"Can't ask for anything more than that," Bryan answered. He brushed his lips against hers one last time.

"But I can," Kelsey chimed in.

Kate put her hands on her daughter's shoulders and turned her around until Kelsey faced the street. She gave her a gentle push toward the smaller of the two cars parked in the driveway.

"Get to school, Kelse. You don't want to be late." And with that, Kate hurried back into the house.

Once inside, she closed and locked the door. In the distance, she heard the sound of first one car and then the other being started up. Bryan and Kelsey were on their way. There wouldn't be any further interruptions, at least for now.

"All right, your father and sister are gone, Trevor," Kate announced as she walked into the living room. Both Trevor and the girl were on the sofa. She noted that the mystery girl acted as if she were sitting on a bed of nails instead of a soft leather sofa. "Can I get either one of you something? Coffee? Tea? Breakfast?"

"Is 'help' on the menu?" Trevor asked.

If she felt any apprehension over whatever was to come next, his stepmother hid it well. "Help is always on the menu, Trevor, you know that. What kind of help do you need?"

"Let me start at the beginning," Trevor offered. In short order, he filled his stepmother in, telling her about how he rescued the woman he'd brought with him and how the trauma of almost drowning had robbed her of her memory.

Kate listened quietly. And when he was finished, she nodded slowly, digesting what he'd told her.

"You're a very lucky girl," she told Venus, squeezing the girl's hand. Her eyes shifted to her stepson. "You both are," Kate emphasized. "They said on the news last night that there was a high tide in force." She closed her eyes for a moment, as if to push the next thought away. "It doesn't take much of an imagination to think of what could have happened. You could have both easily drowned." And then she laughed ruefully. "You'll have to forgive me. That's the mother in me coming out."

Folding her hands before her, she looked up at her stepson. "You said something about needing my help."

He nodded. Although he knew there was nothing he couldn't ask of her, he still hated to impose. "I've got to go in early today. I'm expecting a large lunch crowd and there's the Kellerman anniversary tonight." He still marveled at the idea that two individuals could, within a couple of generations, produce so many people. "A hundred and twenty-nine family members are flying in today to celebrate the anniversary of the two people who started it all and I—"

Kate held up her hand. There was no reason for him to go any further. "Say no more. I can take over." She smiled at the girl sitting so tensely beside her stepson. "I'm not going into the office today, so you caught me at a good time."

Trevor knew better. Even if she were scheduled to go into the office today, Kate would have found a way to re-shuffle her patients in order to be there for him. It was a given. And he adored her for it.

"Thanks. I'd appreciate it if you took Venus to the police station to find out if anyone reported a woman matching her description missing."

Kate glanced from Trevor to the young woman in her living room. Amusement curved her mouth at the name he'd given her. "Venus?"

Venus shrugged a bit self-consciously. No way could she picture herself as the goddess of love. "Since he saved me from the sea," she explained.

Kate nodded. "Like in the painting." Her eyes shifted to her stepson. They made a nice couple, although she doubted if either one of them noticed that. "Okay, you get to work, Trevor, and leave everything else to me."

Relieved and glad to be leaving Venus in such capable hands, Trevor rose from the sofa. Beside him, Venus popped up like toast. "I really appreciate this."

Kate waved away his gratitude. "What's a mother for if not to search for her son's friend's missing identity?" she teased.

"You're the best, Mom." He kissed her cheek, then turned toward Venus. "I'm leaving you in great hands," he told her.

Kate motioned Venus toward Trevor. "Why don't you walk Trevor to the door and I'll go see if I can find you a few things so that you'll have a change of clothes." Her eyes swept over Venus's figure and she made a judgment call. "I think we're the same size." With that, she left the room.

Venus accompanied Trevor the short distance to the front door. She was reluctant to see him go. Right now, he was her oldest friend. She didn't like this clingy side of herself. "You're right, your stepmother seems very nice."

"That's because she is. But she also knows how to get things done," he assured her. "I think she mentioned having a friend at the Bedford police station. That might help move things along. This time tomorrow, you might be home."

Venus forced a smile to her lips. "Great."

But even as she said it, there was no feeling of triumph accompanying the word, no surge of happiness at the thought of going home, even though she had no idea where home was. Instead, she felt a strange foreboding hanging over her. As if home was someplace she ultimately didn't want to be.

But she'd spent all this time being frustrated at not knowing who she was.

Maybe she was just going crazy, Venus thought unhappily.

They were at the front door and her reluctance to see him leave increased almost to the point that she was close to saying, "Don't go." She curbed her impulse and instead, just thanked him.

"Um, I just wanted to tell you that I appreciate your going out of your way like this, enlisting your family to help." Bringing up his family brought something else to mind. Something that had made her curious. "Your sister seemed surprised that you would have brought a woman to the house."

He shrugged, indicating that the matter was inconsequential. "I don't have time to socialize."

"Oh?" Venus looked down at the pullover and jeans he'd given her, as well as the sneakers. "I thought you said that these clothes belonged to a significant other from your past."

Significant other. At one point, that was what Alicia had been to him. What he'd been to her, he was no longer certain. But it was over and he wasn't about to make that kind of mistake again. Heartaches took too long to get over.

"She's gone," he told her, his voice devoid of any feelings. "I'm not much on relationships," he added. "They require even more nurturing than your average soufflé."

He was a chef, all right, she thought, amused at the comparison. "Maybe, but they have a tendency to last a great deal longer than a soufflé if you do them right."

He watched her for a long moment, trying to decide if she was just being philosophical, or remembering something without realizing it. "Are you speaking from experience by any chance?"

The question threw her. She really wasn't sure where this was coming from. The words had just materialized on her tongue.

"I wish to God I knew," she confessed. Venus squinted her eyes, as if that could help her look into herself. It didn't. Finding only another dead end, she shook her head. "I don't think so."

He shouldn't have asked her that. It only aggravated her not to remember, but he'd hoped that a glimmer of a memory had been stirred. Apparently not. "It'll come back to you," he promised again.

He really needed to get going, but something conspired against him in that small foyer, urging him to stay a second longer.

And then another second after that.

For all her bravado, Venus's vulnerability spoke to him. Maybe that was why, just before leaving, he impulsively bent over to kiss her cheek. His intent was just to give her the reassurance of a little gentle human contact. He'd read somewhere that touch offered silent comfort and she needed it.

He hadn't counted on her jumpiness.

Startled, Venus jerked her head. But instead of turning away, she wound up turning her face into his. Which was how it happened.

One second there was only air in that small space, and

the next, her lips were brushing against his. Something seemed to crackle and hiss between them and Venus could have sworn an electrical surge bounded through the atmosphere. Infusing both of them.

She drew in her breath, knowing she should back away. Quickly. But she didn't.

What she did was plant her lips on his in earnest.

And lose herself inside the kiss.

Trevor had no idea how this had mushroomed so quickly. Instead of offering comfort, he was taking it. He found himself cupping the back of her head, his fingers brushing against her face as the friendly, almost impersonal kiss morphed into a great deal more.

It was strong enough to knock his socks off if he hadn't been wearing shoes.

Or maybe even then.

As he went on kissing her, Trevor heard her little moan of pleasure. It vibrated against his lips.

His own pleasure streaked through him. And though his head spun, he was still acutely aware of everything within his surroundings. He was aware of drawing her closer to him. Aware of the tantalizing way her body touched his, setting the tranquil, cool morning on fire.

He was aware of deepening the kiss by inches, slowly so that she wouldn't pull away.

Most of all, he was aware of wanting to do more than just kiss her.

He was aware of wanting her.

Chapter Six

Venus's heart stopped—and then started up again, beating wildly. She'd only meant to say thank you, to kiss him fleetingly because she had no other way to express the gratitude she felt.

She had to admit, she was attracted to him.

She traveled on instinct alone since every other avenue was closed off to her. But now, as she sank further and further into this kiss, she wanted to express gratitude at this heart-pumping turn of events.

While she had no way of knowing for certain, she felt as if she'd never been kissed like this before. Because if she had, the sensation would have struck a chord, jarred loose an avalanche of memories. It would have done *something* other than make her knees buckle.

Survival instincts made her finally pull her head away.

"Sorry," she murmured, taking a step back as she got her bearings. She held on to his forearms for a moment just in case. It took a second for her head to stop spinning and focus. "I didn't mean to get carried away."

Trevor framed her face with his hands, lingering a moment that he really didn't have. Something rather overwhelming had just happened here.

"Nothing to be sorry about," he assured her. "That was very nice, but I've really got to go." There was more than a trace of reluctance in his voice. "But Mom'll take really good care of you."

Venus nodded. She noticed that he went back and forth as to the way he referred to his stepmother. Calling the woman "Mom" instead of "Kate" brought out an even greater degree of warmth in his voice.

"I'm sure she will." Venus suddenly seemed shy. Too shy to be the woman who'd kissed him that soulfully. When she raised her eyes to his face, he felt something in his gut tighten again. Hard. "Will I see you again?"

"Count on it," he promised. "I never leave a project half-finished or a book half-read."

Why did that sound so comforting to her? "Which am I?"

Trevor looked at her for a long moment, fighting the very real, very strong temptation to kiss her again. "A little bit of both," he replied.

He was humming when he left the house.

Ordinarily, once he walked through the door of his restaurant, the outside world didn't exist for him. His only contact with it, other than his patrons, occurred when he had to place his orders for supplies.

But today was different.

Despite the large crowd he anticipated for lunch and his preparations for the Kellerman anniversary banquet, a three-hour party slotted to end at eight because Myra and Jules Kellerman were both in their late seventies and liked to retire at an early hour, his mind kept going elsewhere. He couldn't help wondering how Venus was getting along and if, more important, someone had filed a missing-person's report on her yet.

Was she, even now, remembering another life? The life that had been temporarily lost to her? Was she being embraced by a husband or significant other who'd been frantic with worry about her?

No, Kate would have called him. Wouldn't she?

Trevor quickly went over a set of instructions with some of his staff, then retreated to call home.

But the answering machine picked up.

With an impatient sigh, he shut his cell phone and went back to work. Yet forty-five minutes later had him calling again. With the same results. This time, he called Kate's cell phone. She didn't pick up. Frustrated, he left a message.

He knew he should be rooting for Venus to find her real identity, but a part of him resisted this scenario. The part that'd had its toes curled by her kiss.

Don't get carried away, partner. She could be totally out of your reach, he cautioned himself.

What if she was the married mother of three? What

then? Did she become a fantasy he looked back on in the dead of night when he couldn't sleep?

Hell, what was the matter with him? Trevor shook his head. Since when did he yearn for a relationship? That wasn't his thing. Alicia had taught him well. He didn't have time for a fantasy, let alone a real live woman. His business required every ounce of his concentration, every bit of his time. It was still in the fledgling stage and needed nurturing. Just because the first two years had been profitable didn't mean that he was in a position to coast. Not yet. Perhaps not ever.

He called again in twenty-five minutes. This time, he got Kate instead of her voice mail.

"Hello?"

Finally. He turned away from the kitchen, giving himself a spoonful of privacy. "Hi, it's Trevor. Any luck?"

There was a pause on the other end, as if Kate were trying to connect the dots he'd just scattered before her. "Oh, you mean with finding out who your mermaid is? I'm afraid not." He heard some traffic sounds in the background. "We're on our way home from the police station. There's no missing-person's report out on her, but it might be too soon." Her voice shifted and he had a feeling she was saying this for Venus's benefit as much as his. "Her family might still be trying to find her on their own."

"Yeah, maybe." Or maybe she didn't have a family, he thought. God help him, the thought made him feel oddly light. "Keep me posted, Mom."

"I promise. Oh, and sorry I couldn't pick up the other

times you called. The signal was blocked at the police station for some reason."

"How did you know I called?" He'd only left one message.

"Recent call menu," she answered. Nothing stayed private anymore, he thought. "Oh, and, Trevor?"

He forced himself to focus. "Yes?"

"I think she's a really nice girl," Kate told him warmly.

About to say something to deflect whatever assumptions his stepmother made—and he was fairly certain he knew their nature—Trevor reconsidered.

"Yeah, me, too." There was a crash behind him. Trevor sighed. He didn't have to turn around to know what had just happened. They were right. Good workers *were* hard to find. "Gotta go. The new salad girl the temp agency sent over doesn't realize that she's supposed to hang on to the dishes, not watch them slide off her tray."

Kate laughed and wished him luck before ending the call.

The day seemed three times as long as usual. And within that time frame, anything that could go wrong, did. An order of shellfish somehow suddenly turned into thirty pounds of salmon. He had his second-best man drive over to a fish market to pick up the required shrimp and lobster.

For a while, it was touch and go, but he managed to come through, and by the time the Kellerman banquet was set to begin, everything was in its place down to the white roses woven into the centerpieces on each table.

The affair was such a success that Alice Kellerman Wayne sought him out not once but twice to rave about the dinner.

To Trevor that was always the best part, hearing—and seeing—that he had once again pleased his customers by tantalizing their taste buds. It kept him burning the midnight oil, searching for new ways to improve on tried-and-true recipes and make them his own.

Eventually, the banquet was over and the last of the Kellermans had left the restaurant. The senior Mrs. Kellerman's kiss of thanks was still fresh on Trevor's cheek and warming his heart.

"Nice job, boss," Emilio Juarez, his right-hand man, complimented, coming up to him in the kitchen just as Trevor returned from the reservations desk. "I don't know how you pulled it off, but you did. As always. They looked really happy. I've got a feeling we're going to be seeing more business than we can handle once they start telling their friends what a great spread you put out."

Trevor smiled. "Think so?"

"I'd put money on it—if I were a betting man," Emilio qualified quickly.

"Which you're not," Trevor said, tongue in cheek. Emilio's betting had been a problem for a while, but was now a thing of the past.

"Which I'm not," Emilio answered, raising one hand in a solemn oath. "I gave that stuff up, remember?"

Trevor nodded. He looked at the man, thinking. Emilio was his first in command, his assistant chef. They'd met at the last restaurant that he'd worked in before opening up his own. Emilio struck him as hardworking, quick to learn and a very happy man to have around. Preparing to go off on his own, he'd made Emilio an offer, saying that initially, the pay wasn't going to be as good as what he'd been earning. But he had a chance to get in on the ground floor and once Kate's Kitchen took off, as he was confident it would, then Emilio would be in a very good position. He'd flourish as Kate's Kitchen did.

Left unsaid was the fact that a large preponderance of restaurants closed their doors in less than two years from their starting dates. And Emilio ran the risk of failure. The taint of that tended to stay for a while.

Nonetheless Emilio never hesitated.

"Then we're just going to have to make sure it doesn't fail" was his answer. And it was then that Trevor knew he had picked the right man for the job.

He beckoned his assistant over now. "Emilio, close up for me tonight."

Emilio stared at him as if he'd suddenly lapsed into a foreign language. "Close up?" he echoed.

"Yes."

Emilio still didn't seem to comprehend what was said. "The restaurant?"

Taking out one of the discarded boxes, Trevor repeated, "Yes."

"'Close up' close up?" Emilio repeated. He followed Trevor to one of the preparation tables. "Like, tell everyone to go home and then lock the door?"

"Let them finish eating first," Trevor commented dryly.

Lining the bottom of the box with wax paper, he paused for a moment to address his first assistant. "What's the matter with you? Don't you know how to close up?"

Emilio spread his hands wide. "Sure, but you never let me do it before."

Trevor began putting wedge after wedge of lasagna into the box. "Sure I did."

"No, you didn't," Emilio contradicted. "You're always the last one to go home. Every night," he emphasized. "Eduardo, the bus boy, is convinced you sleep in the refrigerator."

Trevor began putting a second layer on top of the first, separating them with the wax paper. "Tell him I only do that on Tuesdays."

Emilio watched him throw together five very large servings of the Italian dish that had become such a favorite with the customers.

"That's some doggie bag you're putting together," he commented.

Trevor shrugged, trying to make it sound as if this was just business as usual. "I'd thought I'd stop by my parents' house."

Emilio nodded. His expression grew more thoughtful and concerned. "Anything wrong, boss? With your folks, I mean? You don't usually bring them food."

Trevor shook his head. "No, nothing's wrong. I just thought I'd stop by." Boy, that sounded lame, even to his ears.

Emilio eyed the filled cardboard box. "Lot of food for three people."

Trevor debated throwing in a few extra servings and decided to err on the side of caution. Better to have too much than too little. Another foil-wrapped serving joined the others.

"My sister'll probably be home, as well."

"Girls that age don't admit to eating food. I've got five sisters. Trust me, I know."

"Thanks for the advice."

"Tell your folks hi for me. And say it to anyone else, too."

Trevor paused. "Look, if you'd rather not close up—"

Emilio quickly cut him off. "Don't worry about a thing. I know where everything goes. Including you tonight. Have a good night, boss." Emilio put the lid on the box and handed it to his boss. "And try not to worry."

"I wasn't," Trevor told him, taking the heavy box. It was warm to the touch. "Until now."

"Then don't." Emilio opened the back door for him. *"Viva con Dios."*

He understood the Spanish that was the native tongue of some of his staff, but he didn't trust his accent. Like as not, he mangled the words, so instead, he just murmured, "Yeah, you, too."

When he walked in later that evening, Kate met him at the door. The smile on her face was inviting and teasing at the same time. "Well, this is a surprise. I didn't think, after six calls, you'd swing by here, too."

"Five," he corrected.

Kate took the box from him, handing it off to Bryan. "Seven, but who's counting?" she asked cheerfully. And then Kate winked. "She's in the family room, helping Kelsey study."

Trevor was instantly alert. "She remembered something?"

"How to read. She's helping Kelsey run her lines for the play."

He made his way to the family room, then stood just short of the doorway, listening. Outgoing to a fault, Kelsey had had her hand up for every audition since kindergarten. With deliberate dedication, she'd practiced doggedly at perfecting her talent. Over the years, she'd worked her way up from second flower on the right to Dulcinea, the female lead in *Man of La Mancha,* the musical that UCI was putting on this winter.

From the sound of it, his sister had given Venus the part of the misguided Don Quixote. He'd expected something flat and possibly self-conscious coming from Venus. Instead what he heard was confidence, enthusiasm and an extremely pleasant singing voice. He found himself utterly captivated. When Kelsey arrived at a dramatic pause that signaled the end of the scene, Trevor clapped, directing most of the applause toward Venus.

When Venus swung around, surprised at being observed, her cheeks instantly turned to a bright pink hue.

In contrast, Kelsey beamed in response to the applause. His sister took a little mock bow. "Thank you, thank you, I'll be signing autographs in the lobby during intermission."

"The applause was for Venus, Short-stuff," Trevor said, coming into the room. He smiled broadly at the woman with the bright pink cheeks. "She was very good," he continued. "You, you were…" He waffled his hand back and forth to indicate a lukewarm reaction to his sister's performance.

"Just for that—" Kelsey bopped him on the head with her rolled-up script "—I won't mention you when I collect my Oscar." And then she turned toward Venus. "Thanks, that really helped a lot."

Venus carefully closed the script and placed it back on the coffee table where Kelsey kept it. "I'm glad to do it."

"Don't say that," Trevor warned as Venus crossed to him. "You give my sister an inch and she builds a condo on it."

Kelsey sniffed and turned up her nose at him. "Just because you're mean to me doesn't mean everyone else has to be."

"Trevor brought dinner," Kate announced, peeking into the room after having put out five place settings on the kitchen table. "Anyone interested in having their taste buds seduced, come to the kitchen."

Kelsey was already out the door. Venus fell into place beside Trevor and they walked out together. "Sounds too good to pass up," Venus commented, remembering the meal he'd served her last night.

Trevor banked down the temptation of moving off to the side to have her exclusively to himself. "So, how's it going?"

"Well, nobody missed me if that's what you mean." The words were accompanied by a small sigh.

Though he'd asked, he already had the information, thanks to his calls to Kate. He pretended it was news to him. "Maybe whoever the people in your other life are, they don't know you're missing."

She laughed dryly. "Can't have left much of an impression on them, then."

In his opinion, a person would have had to have been dead for a week not react to Venus. But he could see that Kelsey was not-so-covertly watching them, so he kept the remark to himself. The last thing he wanted was for Kelsey to embarrass Venus.

So instead, he cast about for reasons why no one was actively looking for Venus yet. "You could be away on vacation. I found you in the water. Maybe you fell off a cruise ship. Or you were sailing your yacht and accidentally fell off that. If you were alone, nobody would know that you were missing." He gave her an encouraging smile. "There are a lot of explanations why someone wouldn't have filed a missing-person's report on you."

Kelsey got into the spirit of the thing. "Or maybe someone tried to kill you and they think they did," she chimed in with enthusiasm.

"That does it," Bryan announced as he sat down at the table. "No more crime-analysis shows for you, young lady."

Kate placed her hand on top of her husband's. "I don't think you can put a cap on that imagination, honey," she cautioned. She looked around the table. Only Kelsey had helped herself to a serving of lasagna. "Well, come on, I can't be the only one who wants to sample this delicious-looking meal. Venus, take a seat. Help yourself to some dinner." Her eyes narrowed slightly as she shifted her gaze to her son. "You, too, chef."

Though he created things he loved, Trevor rarely felt the desire to partake of his creations. "I never eat what I cook."

"Never?" Venus asked, surprised, as she slid a piece onto her plate.

"Well, hardly ever."

Kelsey, sitting on the other side of Venus, leaned forward so she could see her brother. "That excuse won't fly in court, Trev. So if you're trying to poison us, better say so now."

Shaking his head, he cut into the portion on Venus's plate. As Kelsey watched, he picked up a forkful of the rich Italian fare, put it into his mouth and chewed. Finished, he placed the fork down beside his own empty plate. "Satisfied?"

Kate gestured toward the plate in the center of the table, heaped high with rectangular pieces of sin in melted cheese. "Eat a little more. Chefs are supposed to have some meat on their bones."

Bryan raised his eyes from his plate, momentarily interrupting his own festival of enjoyment. "You're making mother noises again, Kate."

"Sorry, dear. Occupational habit. I'll try to restrain myself, although technically," she continued cheerfully, "no matter how old these two get, I'm still going to be their mother and thus, entitled to make mother noises."

"Only on your birthday, and Christmas," Kelsey requested firmly.

Kate eyed her skeptically. "How about Mother's Day?"

"We'll see," Kelsey promised loftily, then added, "If you've been good."

Kate shook her head and addressed the guest at her table. "And this," she said in mock despair, "is what my daughter calls her best behavior."

"Kelsey wouldn't know 'best behavior' if it came up and bit her," Trevor announced to the room at large.

"You should talk," Kelsey jeered. "Mom told me all about what you and the others used to do when you were kids. Stopping escalators, knocking over mannequins, trying to drag Christmas trees through department stores by their branches."

Listening, Venus's eyes widened with amusement. "Really?"

He didn't want to have to sit and listen to misadventures that had occurred twenty years ago. At least, not in front of Venus. "Kelsey has a tendency to make things up. It's all part of her 'creative' background."

"Mom, back me up here," Kelsey requested.

"Yeah, Mom," Trevor echoed pointedly.

Caught in the middle, Kate chose the diplomatic route. "Trevor and his brothers were…um…spirited," she finally said.

Bryan joined in. "They nearly drove me out of my mind until I found Kate. Went through three housekeepers in a little more than a year."

"That bad?" Venus asked, amused.

"The other women had no stamina," was all that Trevor allowed himself to say.

"Navy SEALs wouldn't have had enough stamina to last around you guys," Bryan said glibly.

Kate leaned over toward Venus and said in a stage

whisper, "My superhero cape is in the hall closet if you'd like to take a look at it later."

"Lies, all lies," Trevor declared, feigning indignation.

As she ate, Venus didn't bother suppressing the smile that came to her lips. The warmth at the table was palpable. She had a feeling she wasn't accustomed to such closeness.

Chapter Seven

A long, contented sigh escaped Kate's lips. She braced her hands before her and leaned back a fraction of an inch.

"Well, if I don't get up now to clear this table," she predicted, "I might just wind up never being able to move again."

Venus was on her feet instantly. "Here, let me help," she offered. Beside her, Trevor rose, ready to join the effort, as well.

But Kate waved them both back down. "No, you're a guest, and you—" she looked at Trevor "—you brought this heavenly fare into our house. You both get to sit this out. However, you and you—" she indicated first her daughter and then her husband "—you two can feel perfectly free to volunteer with the dinner dishes."

Bryan cocked his head, as if getting in tune with his inner self. "Nope, don't feel the need to volunteer at all. There's not even a twinge." He glanced at his daughter. "You feel anything, Kelsey?"

Kelsey shook her blond head adamantly from side to side. "Nope."

"Let me rephrase that. You *will* feel perfectly free to volunteer. Both of you. Now," Kate emphasized, when neither had made a move to get up.

"Just like in the army, they volunteer you," Bryan said to his son with a shake of his head.

"Okay, soldier, march," Kate instructed, playing along with the comparison. "You, too, Private Kelsey. Into the kitchen with both of you." She glanced over her shoulder at the two remaining people seated at the table. "There's a nice moon out tonight. Why don't you two go out on the patio and enjoy it?"

"Could you be more transparent, Kate?" Bryan asked his wife, seeming amused as they walked into the kitchen.

Kate turned on the faucet and began to rinse the dishes off one by one, getting them ready for the dishwasher. "I wasn't trying to be devious, I was trying to get you to leave the two of them alone."

Kelsey set the plates she'd brought in on the counter. "Don't get your hopes up, Mom. Trevor's a workaholic, remember? And after that little stunt that Alicia pulled on him, I don't think he's going to be risking getting involved with anyone else for a long, long time."

Kate grinned. "Your father was a so-called workaholic when I first met him. The Marlowe men are tough nuts to crack—but they do crack," Kate promised. "All it takes is knowing just where to tap."

In the other room, Venus was smiling as she looked at Trevor. "I think that your mother wants us to go outside."

Embarrassed at Kate's less than covert machinations, Trevor said sheepishly, "I'm sorry about that."

"Don't be. She obviously cares about you. I was thinking, while gorging myself on the lasagna, that you could almost feel the love around the table. You've got a really nice family and you're a very lucky man."

As they made their way outside, he couldn't disagree. He'd always known how lucky he was. "Yeah, I suppose I pretty much have it all. Great family I can always depend on and Kate's Kitchen is doing better business than I ever dreamed."

Venus was aware of the glaring omission in his litany of blessings. She tried to make her voice sound conversational as she asked, "Nobody significant in your life?"

He watched her for a long moment. Bits and pieces of thoughts floated through his head. He pushed them aside. "Not at the moment."

Venus nodded. "Which would explain why your mother wanted us out here, moon-gazing." Glancing at Trevor, she saw that he was looking at her and not up at the sky. "You're not gazing up at the moon," she pointed out softly.

"It's just an orb of distant light," he told her. "I'd much rather look at something a little closer to home."

If he wasn't careful, he was going to kiss her again, Trevor thought. And most likely that would leave him open for a myriad of problems down the line. He couldn't believe Venus didn't have someone specific in her life. Someone who was perhaps, even now, moving heaven and earth searching for her. Someone who was going to break down the door at the least opportune time.

He reined in his thoughts again.

"I'd say 'me, too,' but I really don't know for sure," she told him honestly.

For just the evening, he could pretend that she was only the woman he'd rescued from a watery grave, that she knew who she was and that nothing ominous loomed in the background, nothing that would change the truth of this moment. Tomorrow was time enough for reality.

He wanted now. It was all any of them really ever had. "Say it anyway," he encouraged.

Her eyes raised to his. "Me, too."

It took a great deal of effort not to sweep her into his arms when she looked at him like that. "Does it feel right? Does saying the words feel right?" he pressed.

Venus paused for a moment, thinking. "Well, it doesn't feel wrong."

Trevor laughed. "Close enough for now." And then he decided to spread the net a little further. "Nothing coming back to you at all?" he questioned, concerned. "Not even a glimmer all day?"

It frustrated her that her head was still so very empty, that there was nothing to reflect on, nothing to remember that was older than twenty-four hours. Venus lifted a shoulder and then let it drop.

"There've been a couple of flashes, fireflies dashing across my brain," she described, "gone before I can catch them to make anything out of them." She sighed, a wave of anxiety washing over her. Venus pressed her lips together as she turned toward him. "What if I never get my memory back?"

"You will."

He sounded so certain. As certain as she wasn't. "But what if I don't?" she reiterated.

He wasn't accustomed to pessimism. Kate had raised all of them to be optimists, even in the most dire situations. "Then we will handle that when the time comes."

He made it sound so distant, as if giving up hope was something that was rarely done. She liked that about him, she discovered. "And in the meantime?"

"In the meantime," he said, brushing a strand of hair away from her face, "just enjoy the Marlowe hospitality."

She couldn't enjoy herself if she felt she was being a parasite. "I can't just live off your parents, Trevor. It's not right."

"Mom likes helping people and Dad likes seeing Mom happy. From where I'm sitting, there is no problem."

Venus sighed, tucking her hands into the pockets of the sweater Kate had lent her. They had wandered into the middle of the yard, to the fountain that Bryan had given Kate as a tenth-anniversary present. She found the sound of the rushing water soothing.

"I feel like the man who came to dinner." The moment she said the words, her head jerked up and she immediately looked at him, awed and hopeful. "I remembered something," she exclaimed just as Trevor said, "You remembered something."

"What does that mean?" she asked, elated with this bit of information.

The explanation was rather simple. "That either you're the reincarnation of a theater critic or once upon a time, you were an English major at some college. There's no other reason for you to even be acquainted with a play that old."

If that was true about her, it had to be true about him, as well. "Which are you?" she asked.

She was sharp, he thought, pleased. "I minored in English for a little while until I finally admitted out loud that what I really wanted to do was putter around in the kitchen."

"That was some excellent puttering you brought over tonight," she interjected, then said, "I guess I know food, too."

"You've probably eaten once or twice in your life," he speculated, his eyes smiling at her. She was rather adorable, he couldn't help noticing.

"Wise guy." She laughed. Impulsively, she dipped her hands into the fountain, cupped them and then splashed the water in Trevor's direction.

Caught off guard, Trevor cried out in surprise. Surprise turned to active revenge as he reciprocated. Within several seconds, they were both wet, both laughing. And then the laughter slowly died away, giving way to something else. The chemistry that had been hiding in plain sight all evening took center stage.

Before he knew it, Trevor pulled her into his arms. The next moment, he lowered his mouth to hers, kissing her.

Kissing her as if he'd been deprived of oxygen for the last hour and she was his first breath of fresh air.

She tasted sweeter than any dessert he'd ever been inspired to create. He could see himself getting addicted to this, to her, with very little effort.

But the attraction would ultimately lead to a whole lot of trouble, he tried to caution himself, tried to steel himself off from free-falling down the canyon. But he refused to succumb to reality.

He hadn't a clue who she really was. Falling for her, even in a minor way, would completely shake up his well-ordered, moderately uptight world.

Survival mode kicked in belatedly. Trevor forced himself to draw back.

"Sorry." The apology was mumbled and less than half-hearted. "I shouldn't have done that."

"Last I noticed, there were two of us in that kiss." Though she didn't want to, she understood the part that Trevor wasn't saying. That she could, without knowing it, be betraying a husband just by kissing him.

Venus glanced down at her hand. That faint line on the ring finger was still there. But that didn't mean it had been created by a wedding band. Maybe the line had been created by a friendship ring or a family heirloom passed down to her. She couldn't remember.

But if she had a husband, or someone to give her a friendship ring or a family that went along with the heirloom ring, where the hell were they? Why weren't they looking for her? Why hadn't there been anything on the police blotter about a missing twenty-something-year-old?

My God, she realized, she didn't even know how old she was.

Restless, wanting answers, Venus tried to plumb the depths of her soul. Her frustration increased when nothing came. There were no depths to rummage through. For now, what you saw was what you got and it definitely didn't please her.

With a sigh, Venus looked at him. "Shouldn't I have a job or something?"

He considered her question for a moment. "You probably do."

Venus shook her head. "No, I mean…as Venus." She rolled the name he'd given her around on her tongue. It wasn't entirely displeasing or foreign to her. Did that mean he'd accidentally stumbled onto her name? Or was she just getting used to it? Questions, so many questions, and not a single answer. "So that I could begin paying my own way," she explained.

He was about to tell her again that it wasn't necessary. That she needed to focus on finding out who she was before she could find a job, but he changed his mind. An idea came to him, born out of need and the thought that perhaps this way, he would be able to keep an eye on her. This would allow him to be around in case she needed him.

"How are you when it comes to salads?" he asked, watching her reaction.

She didn't understand. "You mean when it comes to eating them?"

"No." He wondered if she was going to be insulted.

Something about her made him think she was a child of privilege. "I mean when it comes to making them."

"I don't know. But it can't be that hard, can it?"

He thought of the girl from the temp agency who'd been sent out today. The girl whose time card he signed as he'd told her that he'd found someone else to fill the position. It was a bold-faced lie. However, even if they had to cut salads out of the menu, there was no way he would allow the temp to continue working for him. He simply couldn't afford to lose that many dishes each day. She didn't seem interested in improving, only in sampling the different foods.

"You wouldn't think so, would you?" he commented dryly.

"What exactly do you have in mind?"

He stated it simply. "I need a salad girl at my restaurant."

She saw through him immediately—or thought she did. "This is charity, isn't it?" Intuition told her that she didn't care for charity, at least when it came to being on the receiving end. However, the word *charity* struck a very distant chord before it faded completely away again.

"No, this is on the level," he assured her. The more he thought about it, the more he liked the idea. "You can ask my parents. I told them that I'd lost my regular salad girl yesterday and that the temp agency I called sent me the salad girl from hell."

Venus laughed. "I didn't know they had salads in hell."

"Only on days like Thanksgiving," he deadpanned, "in place of the turkey."

The grin on her lips spread to her eyes. He could have

sworn he saw laughter in them. And it was infectious. "So, you're saying they celebrate Thanksgiving in hell?"

"No, they feel the lack of it," he told her solemnly, struggling to keep a straight face, "because there's nothing to feel thankful for."

"Except the salad," she teased.

He shook his head, negating her words. "Even that's bad, with rancid lettuce."

"You have rancid lettuce?" The question came from behind them. When he turned to look, Trevor saw that Kelsey was there, standing in the shadows.

"No, and what are you doing out here?" he demanded, crossing to her. "Why aren't you in the kitchen, helping Mom?"

Kelsey bristled slightly at what she perceived to be a veiled reprimand. "It doesn't take that long to load the dishwasher if you're eating takeout."

Takeout. Trevor hadn't thought of the food he'd brought over as common takeout, but he supposed his sister was right. Not that he would ever willingly tell her that.

He gestured toward Venus. "Kelsey, meet my new salad girl."

Kelsey's blue eyes widened in confusion. "Salad girl," she repeated as if trying to find the hidden meaning beneath the phrase. "Is that some kind of new slang term for...?" A mischievous look entered her eyes.

What went on in his sister's brain never ceased to mystify Trevor. "No, Kelsey, that's a position in a restaurant."

Rather than clear things up, his answer seemed to confuse his sister even more. "You're putting her to work?" Kelsey said it as if he'd just chained Venus to an oar and made her a galley slave.

Before he could set her straight, tell her that he was only going along with Venus's wishes, Venus spoke up. "It was my idea," she told Kelsey. "I want to be able to pay my own way, to earn some money." She didn't add that for some reason, it didn't feel right *not* to have any money. She was still working on unscrambling that feeling.

Kate had come out to join them and caught the last part of Venus's sentence. Taking the young woman's hand in hers, Kate looked down at Venus's perfectly manicured fingernails, then turned her hand over slowly, studying it. "My guess is that you don't concern yourself with a paycheck."

Venus's eyebrows drew together quizzically. "You read palms?"

"I notice skin." Kate released her hand. "Yours is as smooth as silk. That means you don't wash dishes and you don't do anything menial. Your nail polish is perfect, which tells me that you just had them done."

Bryan had joined them by now and was shaking his head, an amused expression on his face. "Looks to me like someone else has been watching way too many crime-investigation dramas."

"I study people, not TV shows, honey." Kate patted his cheek affectionately. "You know that. What's this I hear about a job?"

Kelsey opened her mouth, eager to be the source of information, but Trevor beat both her and Venus to the punch.

"I just hired Venus as my new salad girl."

She still wasn't a hundred percent clear on what she was going to be doing. "If I can do the job," Venus qualified.

"A monkey could so do that job—" Kelsey retorted, then realized that her words could be taken as an insult. "No offense," she added hurriedly.

Placing himself in between the two women, Trevor turned to Venus, cutting Kelsey off. "Contrary to my sister's limited knowledge, it takes having a larger brain than a primate to be an actual salad girl."

"Doesn't sound right," Kelsey piped up. "How about salad woman?"

Trevor gave her a dismissive glance. "How about you do your homework?"

"Ever the wit," Kelsey sniffed. She considered herself way too old to be ordered around by one of her brothers. "But you're in luck. As it happens, I do have some."

"Go." He waved her off into the house. "Do it," he encouraged.

Reluctant to leave the small circle, Kelsey sighed and retreated into the house.

Kate took the opportunity to move closer to Venus. She slipped her arm through the other woman's. "You know, you really don't have to find a job. You're free to stay here as long as you need to."

Venus smiled at her. "That's really very generous of you. Of both of you," she added, her gaze taking in Bryan, as well. "But I'd feel better if I was paying you something."

Kate had always known when to back off. "Well, as long as it makes you feel better, I guess I can't argue with that."

Hearing his wife's declaration, Bryan could only

laugh. "Sure you can, honey." He wrapped one arm around his wife's waist. "You could argue with anyone, anytime, anyplace—and most likely win hands down. I should have made you join the firm."

"I'd rather just join you," Kate said, pausing to kiss her husband's cheek. She nodded at the glass in his hand. It was half-full with something that looked half amber, half some sort of hazy mixture. "Make me one of those. Better yet, show me how." Even as she said it, she was taking his hand in hers and pulling him back into the house.

Within a few seconds, Trevor found himself alone again with Venus.

"Still not too subtle, Mom," Trevor called after Kate.

"I haven't the slightest idea what you're talking about," she replied, raising her voice so that it carried as she continued walking into the house. "I just want your father to show me how to make one of those drinks he likes."

"Not much mystery to making a rum and Coke," Trevor commented more to Venus than to Kate.

Venus was smiling. Whether at him, or because of Kate's actions, he didn't know. All he knew was that it was like watching a magnificent sunset.

Chapter Eight

Kate glanced up from the coffeemaker when Venus walked into the kitchen the next morning. The smile on the young woman's face as she uttered a greeting was more a veiled grimace. Motherly instincts immediately rose to the surface.

Abandoning the coffee she was preparing, Kate crossed over to Venus. "Are you all right?"

Venus splayed her hand over her unsettled abdomen. "I'm having…" More frustration assaulted her as she searched for the description in vain. "Oh, what's the word?"

Kate noted the way Venus pressed her hand to her stomach. "Butterflies?" she guessed.

She wasn't sure that was the word. But beggars

couldn't be choosers. "As good a word as any, I guess," Venus said. "Except that they feel a lot bigger."

Kate smiled as if she were familiar with the feeling. "No need to be nervous."

"I'm not sure if I've ever had a job before," she confessed. She watched as Kate returned to the coffeemaker and poured out a cup of the dark liquid. "Nothing's coming to me." Kate handed her the cup and Venus wrapped her hands around it. The warmth worked its way through her fingers and soothed her. "What if I mess up?" She took a sip and let the black liquid wind its way through her slowly. "What if I disappoint Trevor?"

Kate poured a cup for herself, adding in a generous allotment of milk and sugar, then sat down across from Venus. "The last thing you need to worry about is disappointing Trevor."

Venus frowned into her cup. "What makes you say that?" She would have given *anything* to be sure about at least one thing. Right now, everything felt like a huge question mark, including her.

"I know my boys," Kate answered. "Trevor's the patient one." She didn't add that she'd seen the way Trevor had looked at her when he thought no one else noticed. Didn't say how she hoped Trevor could become involved in something other than mixing several ingredients together in a bowl or pot. "He doesn't expect you to be the world's greatest salad girl right off the bat. You've got until at least the end of the day." And then she laughed when she saw the unnerved expression that entered Venus's eyes. Rising from her stool, Kate gave her a quick hug with her free hand. "I'm kidding."

And then, the crystal sugar bowl at Venus's elbow told her that, "She does that kidding around stuff to make you feel better, you know."

Venus's eyes widened as she stared at the bowl on the table. "The sugar bowl, it just—"

"Talked?" Trevor asked, walking into the kitchen through the back door.

Because of the time, he'd assumed that the family was still at breakfast. Parking his car at the curb, he'd circled the house and made use of the back entrance. Venus looked pretty, he thought. Pretty and scared. He had a feeling that the talking sugar bowl had nothing to do with that.

Seeing Trevor, Venus slid off the stool and was quick to join him.

"Yes," she breathed in relief.

"I take it that my mother forgot to mention the little fact that she's a ventriloquist." He glanced at Kate, shaking his head.

"Actually, the subject never came up," Kate responded innocently. And then her eyes sparkled as, for a moment, she entertained a fond memory. She patted Venus's hand before turning back to the stove and the French toast she was preparing. "That's how I caught his father's attention."

"Your ability to make words come out of inanimate objects was the *second* thing that caught my attention, Kate," Bryan interjected, striding into the kitchen like a man who had no time to sit down and eat breakfast like a normal person. If anything, he appeared to debate grabbing something on the run.

"What was the first?" Kelsey asked. She was a couple of steps behind him.

Once in the kitchen, she made a beeline for the counter, eyeing the French toast like someone who hadn't eaten for at least a month.

"Please," Kate said, rolling her eyes and then glancing in Bryan's direction. She deposited a traveling mug filled with coffee into his hands. "Not in front of the children."

"I don't see any children here," Kelsey quipped, making a show of looking from her brother to Venus and then down at herself. "Spill it, Dad."

Bryan grinned fondly. "Your mother looked delicious in jeans. Back in those days, my life was so hectic, I'd forgotten that I could be anything but a lawyer and a father."

"A father and a lawyer," Kate corrected. Dusting the first two pieces of French toast with powdered sugar, she wrapped them up in wax paper and deposited them into a paper bag, along with two napkins. "The kids always came first," she explained tactfully.

Time to go before they got bogged down in nostalgia, Trevor thought. He glanced at Venus. "So, you ready to blow this three-ring circus?"

"It's not a three-ring circus until you meet Trent, Travis and Mike," Bryan told his houseguest as he accepted the paper bag from his wife.

"Don't forget Miranda," Kelsey added. She stood waiting for the next serving of French toast to make its way off the griddle.

"Miranda?" Venus asked. This was a new name for her—or had she missed it before? "Who's Miranda?"

"Mrs. Mike," Kelsey informed her. "Or she will be as soon as they get married. You like weddings, Venus?" Kelsey asked, moving in closer to her parents' house-guest. "Because I'm trying to convince them to have one big blowout of a wedding, but Mike likes things to be on the quiet side and—"

Trevor saw Venus grow extremely pale and her eyes appeared to glaze over. "Kelsey, stop talking," Trevor ordered.

Bristling at being ordered around in front of company, Kelsey immediately went on the defensive. "Why? I can talk in my own house if I wa—"

Trevor waved her into silence without looking in her direction. His attention was riveted on Venus. Instead of snapping out of it, she seemed even further away than she had a moment ago. "Venus?" He took hold of her hand, hoping that the contact would bring her around. "Are you all right?"

She couldn't make out the words. It was all she could do to hear his voice. Everything around her had retreated until it felt miles away, taking the light with it.

And then suddenly, disembodied bits flashed through her mind. The word *wedding* resounded in her brain as if it were in a large echo chamber.

In one of the flashes, she thought she saw a wedding

dress. Her wedding dress. Or was that a picture in a magazine?

She felt hot and cold at the same time.

And sick to her stomach.

There were hands, gentle hands, catching her. Was she falling? Through the air? Into the water?

Suddenly, she felt something wet against her mouth. The ocean? Venus gasped, afraid that her next breath might be her last.

And then things began to slip back into focus.

She was on a chair, sitting at the table in a bright, sunny kitchen. People were gathered around her. Strangers, talking at her.

No, wait, not people, not strangers. Trevor. The man who'd saved her. Who'd dived into the water and risked everything so that she didn't sink to the bottom of the sea, forever disappearing without a trace.

Trevor.

"Oh God," she gasped again, throwing her arms around his neck. Her heart hammered wildly in her ears as anxiety crackled and raced through her. But why? She hadn't a clue.

"What?" Trevor cried, holding her to him as he crouched beside her chair. "What is it? You're shaking like a leaf." She'd started shaking when Kelsey tried to give her some water. He ordered his sister back. "Put the glass of water down, Kelsey. For some reason, it triggered something for her."

"Maybe you should lie down," Kate suggested gently to a still very pale Venus.

Venus drew in a deep breath, trying to steady herself. She felt like a fool, drawing this much attention. Especially since she couldn't explain what had just happened.

"No, I'm fine." She looked up at Kate. "I'm sorry. I don't know what came over me. It's just that, suddenly, I wasn't here anymore."

"Where were you?" Bryan prodded.

She raised her eyes to the older man's face. "I don't know," she confessed honestly. She hated this helpless feeling. "It all just kind of swirled together." She turned her head to look at Trevor. "I thought I remembered something and then it just sucked me away."

"But to where?" Kelsey wanted to know.

"Leave her alone, Kelse," Trevor told his sister. He was still kneeling beside Venus's chair, where he had lowered her when she looked about to faint. "It doesn't matter where."

"Maybe you're trying too hard to remember, dear," Kate said softly. "Don't force it. These things take time." Especially if it involved a repressed memory, Kate thought. Which this obviously did. "It'll come back to you if it's meant to."

"What do you mean by that?" Trevor asked.

"The mind protects us," Kate told her stepson. "It draws a curtain around what it feels we can't handle. She'll remember things when she's better equipped to deal with them."

Did that mean that someone had tried to kill her? Trevor wondered. He couldn't think of any other reason for her to be in the water that night. She'd either leaped from a vessel, trying to escape, or someone had thrown her overboard.

"Do you really think so?" Venus asked. She desperately wanted to remember something, any little clue to who she really was.

"I'd believe her if I were you," Bryan confided. "In my experience, she's hardly ever wrong." He ended his statement with a wink.

It made her feel better. Venus nodded, then, taking another deep breath, she rose to her feet. "I'm sorry." Her apology took in everyone in the room. "I didn't mean to make a scene."

Kate waved away the apology. "You didn't. We're just glad you're all right."

Venus turned toward Trevor. "We'd better get going."

He wasn't altogether certain that was still a good idea. "Maybe you should stay home today," he suggested. "You can get started tomorrow."

"By tomorrow, my butterflies will be condors. And you'll be short who knows how many salads. No, I'm okay, really." She could see he wasn't convinced. "Please, Trevor, I want to work. I want to be busy, be helpful."

Trevor had more than his share of doubts about the wisdom of letting her start working. He looked over her head toward Kate, silently asking her opinion. As a psychologist who dealt with children, she was the closest thing to a doctor they had.

"If she thinks she's up to it, let her try," Kate counseled.

He still wasn't completely convinced, but he found he had trouble saying no when Venus looked at him like that—with liquid green eyes that pleaded so eloquently. So he sighed and nodded.

"You heard the lady," he said, nodding toward his mother. "Let's get going."

He was rewarded with a wide, relieved smile and a whispered, "Thank you."

"Don't thank him until you find out what he's paying you," Kelsey called after them.

Trevor purposely brought Venus into the restaurant more than an hour before the rest of the staff was due. He wanted to use the time to go over things with her, to orient her to her surroundings and make her as comfortable as possible. In his opinion, there was nothing worse than feeling uncertain about what you were doing, knowing that at least a dozen pairs of eyes were covertly, and not-so-covertly, watching you.

"There's really not much to it," he assured her after reviewing the ingredients of the five basic side salads Kate's Kitchen served: chef, Caesar, Greek, cob and the house salad, which was a mixture of the best of the other four, doused with four kinds of cheeses. "I guarantee that you'll be doing these in your sleep by the end of the day."

She nodded, her mouth curving in a smile that wasn't a hundred percent confident. But she did appreciate the fact that Trevor had confidence in her—and that he had hired her on in the first place. "I want to thank you for letting me do this."

"I'm not 'letting' you do anything," he corrected. "You're

bailing me out. I need a salad girl—or woman if you prefer," he amended, remembering Kelsey's terse correction.

"What I prefer is not to let you down," she told him, looking at the array of ingredients spread out before her on the table.

"Not a chance," he told her with a wink that went straight to her stomach and created havoc amid the butterflies.

If she was about to say something, she never got the chance, because at that minute Trevor heard the back door being opened. The next moment, Emilio came walking in. The all but perpetual smile on the young Latino's face widened when he saw someone else in the kitchen.

"Hey, who's the new girl?" Emilio called out as he made straight for them.

Protectively, Trevor glanced at Venus's face to make sure that his assistant didn't overwhelm her. Emilio had a tendency to come on pretty strong right from the first moment.

Trevor refrained from putting his arm around her. "This is Venus."

"Venus," Emilio repeated, rolling the name over on his tongue. His dark eyes took instant measure of her and it was obvious that he didn't find her lacking in any department. "Beautiful name," he told her, then asked, "Venus what?"

Venus looked toward Trevor for help. They'd never come up with a last name, even for simplicity purposes. "Just Venus," Trevor told his assistant.

"Well, 'Just Venus,' I'm 'Just Emilio.'" He took her hand and rather than shaking it, he brought it up to his lips and pressed a kiss against her skin.

"And, if you don't want to be 'just laid off,' I suggest you 'lay off,'" Trevor informed his assistant with just a touch of seriousness beneath the cheerful warning. He draped his arm across the shorter man's slim shoulders and drew him away from the preparation table. "Make five of each, Venus. I'll get back to you later," he promised. "You," he said, addressing Emilio, "come with me."

Emilio offered no resistance. "Well, well, well," he declared with a wide, blinding grin as he appraised his employer. The three identical words hung in the air like bursts of gunfire in suspended animation.

Over in the corner now, Trevor glanced at his assistant, struggling to curb his impatience. This was something new for him. Ordinarily, patience was all but his middle name.

"What's that supposed to mean?" he inquired.

Emilio considered Trevor a friend as well as his employer. Sometimes, the lines became a little blurred.

"Acting a little territorial about the help, aren't you?" He cocked his dark head, amusement shining in his eyes as he studied Trevor's face. "Something interesting going on between you and 'Just Venus'?"

Trevor did his best to seem as if he wasn't emotionally invested in Venus any more than with his other employees.

Shrugging, he replied, "It's a very unique situation."

That only seemed to spark more interest in his assistant. Leaning against the wall, Emilio crossed his hands before his chest, like a man who had all day to shoot the breeze.

"Do tell."

Knowing Emilio's reputation as a lover, Trevor felt that a warning was in order. "And if you put the moves on her, I might just have to quarantine you in the walk-in freezer."

Emilio looked as if he was vindicated. And delighted.

"So, she *does* light your fire. I didn't think there was a woman alive who did that. Good for you," Emilio declared, clapping him on the back. "I've gotta say, I had my doubts about you for a while, but when you pick 'em, you sure pick 'em."

He didn't bother asking what the other man meant by "doubts." There was no time to get into a discussion and he knew that Emilio could go on talking for hours. Trevor cut to the heart of the matter.

"Nobody's 'picking' anyone." He lowered his voice, his manner indicating that he didn't want this to become general knowledge, that he was sharing something with his assistant and not the immediate world. "Venus has amnesia."

Emilio looked in Venus's direction. She was busy making the salads as Trevor had requested and seemed not to realize that she was under scrutiny. "For real?"

"Yes, 'for real.'"

Emilio frowned slightly, as if he had trouble wrapping his mind around the concept.

"She tell you this during the job interview?"

"She 'told' me this after I pulled her out of the ocean the other night." He hadn't wanted to talk about it because it made him seem like a hero and he had no desire for that kind of attention. But neither did he want to lie, especially not to someone he worked so closely with. "She was drowning."

Emilio's eyes lit up with genuine admiration. "Hey man, you're a hero—"

Trevor cut him short. "That's not why I'm telling you this. I want you to keep an eye on her, help her out if she needs it."

Emilio nodded his head, as if that went without saying. And then an impish grin curved his lips. "Times this rough that you've gotta pluck people out of the ocean to come work for us?"

The rhythmic sound of a knife chopping its way through celery provided background music as they talked. "Working was her idea. She doesn't want to be a parasite—her words."

Emilio nodded. "Says something about her character," he commented, then his eyes lit up again, as if a pleasing thought had entered his mind. "Say, where's she staying? 'Cause you know, my place's pretty large and—"

Trevor knew that Emilio was honorable enough if the occasion demanded it, but what his assistant was about to suggest still echoed of leaving the fox in charge of guarding the henhouse. Again, he cut Emilio short. "Already taken care of."

A knowing grin split his face. "Stashed her at your place, huh?"

"No," Trevor informed him. "She's staying with my parents."

Emilio shook his head. "Makes things kind of hard," he empathized.

"Makes things aboveboard," Trevor countered. He didn't want the man getting the wrong idea—or promoting it around the kitchen. "I'm just helping out a fellow human being."

Emilio laughed at the protest. "If you think that's a fellow, I'm sending you to my sister's eye doctor right now."

Trevor gave him a look. There were dishes to prepare. "Get to work, Emilio."

Emilio saluted with a flourish. "You got it, boss." If his grin was any wider as he walked away, it would have made him too top-heavy to move.

Chapter Nine

Anxious and hopeful. This was what a parent probably felt like on his child's first day in nursery school. Trevor had observed Venus off and on throughout the day.

His feelings for Venus weren't exactly parental in nature. But he had to admit that his concern about her ability to handle the job was greater than the impact that messing up might have on his restaurant's reputation.

For once, that was only a minor concern.

He found himself desperately worried that if she couldn't handle what she was doing, if she performed the job poorly, Venus would feel bad about it.

He didn't want her feeling bad.

He needn't have worried.

Venus might not know her way around her own mind,

but when it came to the kitchen, the woman he'd pulled from the ocean was apparently a born natural. And what she didn't know, others on his staff were eager to help her with. Everyone, from the soup chef to the pastry chef and all the people in between, was more than willing to lend the "new girl" a hand, impart advice or just shoot the breeze with her.

He'd picked a good crew, Trevor thought with satisfaction. They had far more in common with one big happy family than a collection of diverse people who had to work hard not to get in each other's way. All this while doing what they did best in the hottest area of the restaurant.

And Venus appeared to be an excellent addition to this mix.

"You did good," he told her after the last order had been filled. They began to shut down the kitchen, putting everything back in its proper place where it would remain until the following morning.

Venus smiled, exhausted more by the attack of nerves she'd waltzed around with all day than the actual work. She felt both tired and wired at the same time.

"It did go pretty well, didn't it?" Her feet were killing her. But it was a small price to pay for the way she felt. "At least there were no accidents," she said proudly.

Trevor smirked, amused. "Were you expecting any?"

Emilio had told her how long her predecessor had lasted and why she'd been let go. "I'd be lying if I said I wasn't worried about knocking things over, dropping an entire tray of salads on the floor," she answered.

Emilio was to blame for that, Trevor thought. He was likable, a quick study and he worked hard, but he never knew when to stop talking. "Luckily, we don't require our salad girl to balance an entire tray of salads with one hand until just before her first paycheck is cut," Trevor quipped.

Just then, Emilio entered the kitchen carrying a tray of half-empty condiment containers. He set it down on the first flat surface he came to. "Hey, boss, if you want to take Venus here home, I can lock up again," Emilio volunteered. "Like last night."

"That's okay, I wouldn't want to put you out two days in a row," Trevor deadpanned. The truth of it was, he didn't want to seem lax in his responsibilities. That would be all that Emilio needed to start ribbing him.

Emilio downplayed it as if the matter didn't faze him. "Whatever you say, boss. But if you ask me, it seems a shame to waste a perfectly good moon just because you always have to be the last one going out the door." Turning on his heel, Emilio shook his head and began to walk slowly toward the door. So slowly, Trevor observed, that if it was any slower, the man would have been walking backward.

Venus moved in front of him. "Can I do anything to help?"

Amused by just how slowly Emilio could actually walk, he didn't immediately follow the gist of Venus's offer. "With?"

"Locking up." She gestured around the kitchen. "Making it go faster."

Was that her way of saying that she wanted to get home? "Tired?"

"No." She shook her head so hard that the ends of her hair bounced. "I just want to help. I think I'm on an adrenaline high right now."

Trevor's eyes crinkled as he laughed. "I've never heard a salad girl say that to me before. Hey, Emilio," he called out, raising his voice.

Still not at the door, his assistant spun around on a dime and crossed back to him in a flash. "At your service, boss."

The man would have never made it as a secret agent, Trevor thought. He was utterly transparent. "Maybe I will let you lock up again tonight."

"Knew you'd see it my way." Emilio's wide, satisfied grin turned softer and more appreciative as his eyes shifted toward Venus. "See you tomorrow, Venus. Good job today. Really," he underscored.

"Thank you," she murmured just before she fell into step beside Trevor. A sense of triumph echoed through her. She liked the way it felt. Liked being productive and part of a team. Venus turned her face up to Trevor. "Everyone's so nice here. You must love coming in to work."

"It has its moments," he allowed. Trevor got the door and held it open for her. A gust of warm wind greeted them both the moment they stepped outside the shelter of the restaurant. Trevor sighed. "Looks like the Santa Ana winds are back."

Venus wrapped her arms around herself. Rather than the customary hot winds that blew in from the desert, this breeze felt cool. She took a deep breath, unconsciously testing the air.

"I hope the fires don't start up," she said with feeling,

then stopped abruptly when she saw Trevor looking at her. She couldn't quite read his expression. "I remembered something else, didn't I?"

"That you did." He ushered her over to his car. There weren't very many left in the restaurant's parking lot at this time of night. "It won't be long now before the rest of your life comes catching up to you and you remember everything."

The thing was, Trevor thought as he opened the passenger side of his vehicle for her, even though he made himself sound encouraging for her sake, he wasn't altogether sure he was really rooting for her memory to return.

Because with the return of her memory, quite possibly, a completely different woman might emerge than the one he became more and more captivated by.

A routine began to fall into place. Trevor would pick Venus up every morning at his parents' house and bring her back there each evening. And in between, he mentored Venus. The routine seemed to evolve naturally.

Initially, he noted that she was covertly observing him during work hours, watching him not just prepare different dishes, but create things when he felt the spirit move him. When he would catch her, she'd look away, pretending that she hadn't been staring at his every move. After the third time, he'd motioned her over.

"Would you like to learn how to make this?" he asked, "this" being stuffed manicotti.

She never hesitated. "Yes."

He began teaching her then and there. Right from the

beginning, Venus soaked up his words like a thirsty flower that had been neglected and left out in the sun far too long. After that, he took it upon himself to encourage her to experiment, to test out new recipes according to her tastes during the time when their doors were closed between lunch and dinner.

As a result of his supportive nature and praise, Venus showed her creativity and he and Venus got even closer.

If Venus was having any more flashes from the past, like the one she'd had in his parents' kitchen just before her first day of work, she made no mention of it. Rather than desperately try to discover her identity, she seemed to be more interested in growing, in doing her job while continually learning about cooking as a form of art from their daily classes.

She'd never been happier.

And maybe that was the problem. Maybe that was why she couldn't remember anything. Because the state of her old life had been too horrible to recall. She doubted she could have been this happy in her other life. If she had, she reasoned, wouldn't there be this driving need to reconnect? Wouldn't something inside her be fighting to surface? To bring about a return to what had once been?

Since there wasn't, she drew her own conclusions that the life she'd led before had left her unhappy and unfulfilled.

And definitely not like the life she currently led. Here she felt warm and happy, cared for, not just by Trevor, but by everyone in his family. Even by the people at the restaurant.

It didn't get much better than this, she mused, watching the dark scenery go by her window as Trevor drove her home.

Even that felt right, thinking of the Marlowes' home as her own. It was as if she'd been missing pieces of herself all this time and they were just now finally showing up.

She'd be complete soon.

A month passed and then another. It was more like a lifetime. A happy lifetime. Venus knew in her heart she should be making more of an effort to try to remember who she was, and she felt guilty because she wasn't. But in all honesty she grew less and less interested in finding out who she'd been. A part of her feared that knowing who she was would ruin what she had now. So, stubbornly, she lived in the moment and relished each one that she had. Not just the time she spent each day with Trevor, but with his family, as well. The ones she'd met so far.

The only tribute to the past was the rock-solid feeling that she'd never experienced anything like this before. Never known this kind of contentment, never experienced this sense of belonging.

It created enough of an argument for her not to remember. The prospect of remembering no longer held any allure, only fear.

She was more than content to remain Venus for the rest of her days.

"Venus, do you mind getting that?" Kate called out from the kitchen where she and Trevor were putting together a spectacular Sunday dinner. Only at the last minute had it been transformed into a prewedding meal honoring the soon-to-be married couple. "I think I hear someone pulling up the driveway."

Presently alone in the living room because Kelsey was still upstairs and Bryan was in his study, Venus sailed to the front door and pulled it open.

The next moment, she stopped dead and stared.

She would have asked Trevor why he'd suddenly decided to change his clothes—except that there were two of him. And they were both coming up the front walk. Utterly amazed, she looked from one to the other. They were perfect copies of one another. And Trevor.

"My God," she whispered, "you really do look identical."

"And you must be Venus," the closer one to her, Trent, said warmly. "Trevor's mermaid," he added with an amused grin. Both his hands enveloped hers. He was staring at her as much as she was at him. "Mom said you were a knockout."

Venus cleared her throat self-consciously. She'd hardly heard a word of what the man in front of her said.

"I'm sorry, I don't mean to stare," she confessed. "It's just that—my God, you're complete clones of one another…." Her voice trailed off in wonder.

Travis grinned. "That's okay, we're used to it."

"Used to it?" Trent echoed, amazed at the tame reference to their past. "We would take advantage of it any chance we got." He helped himself to one of the bottles of beer that Kate had put out. "Taking each other's tests because Travis was better at math than I was and I was better at English lit." Twisting the top off, he took a long swig.

They'd piqued her curiosity. "What was Trevor better at?"

"Not cheating," Trevor answered, walking into the room with a tray of hors d'ouevres. He placed the tray down on the side table and nodded toward his brothers. "I see you've met my clones."

"Just because you were born half a minute earlier doesn't make us your clones," Travis said. He paused to pop a stuffed mushroom cap into his mouth. Anything else he was about to add was temporarily forgotten as the taste transformed him. "My God, but you do know your way around a kitchen." He shook his head in wonder. "This is damn terrific, Trev." He went to take more.

"Leave some for the rest of us," Trent warned. He appeared ready to slap away Travis's hand. Looking over toward Venus, he grinned. "That's our Trevor. Someday, he's going to make some lucky person one hell of a wonderful wife."

"Just because you don't know a mushroom from a toadstool—" Trevor began, only to be waved into silence by Kelsey as the latter entered the room. His sister went straight to their houseguest, playfully hooking her arm through Venus's.

"Creepy, isn't it?" she commented. "Their looking so alike. If they were dressed alike, you probably couldn't tell them apart."

"I could pick out Trevor."

The statement came with no bravado or fanfare. It was a simple given.

"How?"

She'd had more than one opportunity to study Trevor, up close and personal. "Well, for one thing, Trevor's smile is higher on the left than on the right. And when he's lost in thought, one eyebrow rises higher than the other."

"Is she right?" Trent cocked his head. "Smile for us, Trev."

"Or think," Travis chimed in, more than a little amused by Venus's observation.

"Yes, she's right," Kate announced as she crossed to the table from the kitchen. She deposited the basket of warm rolls onto the table, placing them near Bryan's plate because she knew how much he liked crisp French bread straight out of the oven. "That was one of my markers when I first came to work here," she confided to Venus. "They were determined to fool me and I was just as determined to see them for the individuals they were. I won," she added in case there was any doubt.

"Lucky for you they weren't quadruplets," Kelsey quipped, selecting the largest mushroom cap she could find. It disappeared behind her lips in less than a heartbeat.

"Mike looked enough like them to almost make that happen," Kate told her, still recalling her first encounter with the Marlowe boys—before they became hers. "He was just a tiny bit taller—"

"And not as charming," Travis interjected, helping himself to a third mushroom. Or maybe it was his fourth.

"I don't know if I'd exactly call what you guys were like then 'charming,'" Bryan said, finally joining them.

"A challenge," Kate told Venus with a fond, nostalgic smile. "They were definitely a challenge." There was love in her voice as she said it.

Not for the first time Venus was struck by how close-knit, how warm they all were. And how foreign that seemed to feel to her, even though, at the same time, she found it incredibly comforting. And alluring.

Not knowing a single detail about herself, she still sensed that her family had been nothing like these people, who all cared about each other and could still take in a stranger and make her feel welcome. Maybe she didn't even have a family, she mused. For a second, curiosity flared again, but then she banked it down. She wanted nothing marring this special event.

"So where's the couple of honor?" Kelsey asked, dramatically looking at her watch. "Aren't they supposed to be here by now? I mean, this dinner is for them, right?"

"This dinner is for all of us," Kate told her daughter tactfully.

"But most especially for them." Kelsey stood by her assessment. "They're late."

Trent's mouth curved in a wicked smile. "Maybe they got distracted."

"Distracted or not, they'll be here if they know what's good for them," Trevor commented, walking over to the window that faced the street. He drew back the curtain and gazed out.

"Right," Travis deadpanned, nodding his head. "Can't miss a meal created by Trevor the Magnificent."

Trevor dropped the curtain as he looked over his shoulder at Travis. "Well, at least you've finally got my name right."

Venus glanced from one brother to the other. "Are they always like this?" she asked Kate.

Kate set down the large covered dish that contained the main course, something that Trevor had spent several hours putting together. She nodded. "Pretty much so. Although," she added, recalling the early days of her arrival in this house, "there was a time when they were very introverted. I could hardly get them to talk. Turned out they were testing me. This is much better," she assured Venus.

Helping himself to a bottle of stout, Bryan sighed and shook his head. "If you say so, Kate."

"Men," Kate whispered fondly to Venus. "What do they know?" And then she raised her head, listening. "Trevor—" Kate looked over at her co-chef "—be a dear and bring out the mashed potatoes from the kitchen. I hear someone pulling up in the driveway."

Cocking her head, Venus strained to hear the sound of a running engine, or at least one rumbling into silence as it was turned off. She heard nothing. Kate, she thought, had phenomenal hearing.

"What if it's not them?" she asked.

"Then we'll invite whoever it is," Kate replied cheerfully.

Venus knew Kate was serious. She also realized that she liked the woman's answer because it spoke of a hospitality that was without bounds. She had a feeling people like Kate were scarce in the world she couldn't remember and had less and less of a desire to reclaim.

Losing her memory, she decided, might turn out to be the luckiest thing that had ever happened to her.

Chapter Ten

"Well, looks like two down and three to go," Kate commented as she turned the faucet up to fill the sink with sudsy, warm water.

"There's more food?" Bryan asked, looking around the kitchen. He groaned as he held the sides of his stomach. "I'm not sure if I can do justice to any more—"

"No, not food, Bryan." She laughed. "Kids." Reaching for a towel, Kate wiped off her hands. The dishes needed to soak for a while. "I was talking about our children pairing off."

Bryan's dark eyebrows drew together in a thoughtful squiggle. "Two? What two?"

She began with what he knew. "There's Mike and Miranda."

Bryan nodded. "Right."

And then she smiled as she added, "And Trevor and Venus."

"Hold it right there. There's nothing going on between Trevor and Venus," he insisted. "Besides, the woman doesn't even know who she is."

"Small matter," Kate said, brushing off his statement. Affection came into her eyes as she looked at her husband. "And if you think there's nothing going on between them, you're just as sweetly naive—and blind— as the first day I came to work for you."

He bristled at the label. His was a sharp legal mind trained to think on multiple levels. There was nothing naive or blind about it—or him. "Trevor's just helping the girl out, Kate, that's all."

Kate sank all four glasses into the bubbles. They went down without a trace.

"I didn't say he wasn't. I also don't think 'that's all.'" She emphasized the phrase that he'd used. "Look at the way Trevor watches her when he thinks no one's noticing."

He was beginning to think that women were preprogrammed to see romance everywhere. "Oh? And just how is he looking at her?"

Kate couldn't resist patting his face. "The same way you used to look at me." Turning away, she added silverware to the water.

Amused, Bryan asked, "And how did I look at you?"

She closed her eyes for a moment, remembering. There was nothing like the thrill of discovering that romance had entered your life. "Like I was the light of your life."

Bryan came up behind her, slipping his arms around her waist and nuzzling her neck. "You still are, Kate."

"Oh, God, get a room, you two," Kelsey cried, pretending to avert her eyes as she came in with an empty serving dish.

"We did," her father told her, leaving his arms around his wife for a moment longer. "As a matter of fact, we got a whole house. Speaking of rooms, why don't you go to yours?"

"I just came in to see if Mom needed any help," Kelsey replied, innocence personified.

"She asks once she knows that everything was taken care of," Bryan said in a deliberate narrative voiceover.

Kelsey spread her hands wide. "Hey, I can't help it if I have great timing." She glanced at the Roman numerals on the kitchen clock that hung over the table. "I'm going to go back to the school library. I've got this nasty paper due next week and I haven't even gotten started yet."

A small laugh escaped Bryan's lips. "Why doesn't that surprise me?"

Taking her purse, which had been left slung over the back of one of the chairs, she slipped it on her shoulder. "Don't wait up," she told them.

Kate frowned slightly, her mind already into overdrive. "Be careful, Kelsey."

One hand on the doorknob, Kelsey paused to sigh dramatically. "Mom, this is Bedford. Nothing ever happens in Bedford."

"There's always a first time," Kate pointed out. And

then she glanced toward the living room. "By the way, is Trevor still here?"

"Nope." Kelsey grinned as if she was the gatekeeper of a provocative secret. "And neither is Venus."

Kate exchanged looks with her husband. They both looked at Kelsey for enlightenment. "Oh?"

"Trevor mentioned that he had gotten an aquarium and Venus said she wanted to see it. She thinks she remembers liking fish, but she couldn't be sure," Kelsey said over her shoulder as she went out the back door.

"Aquarium," Bryan repeated, slowly examining the word. "Is that anything like 'come see my etchings?'"

Kate only smiled, feeling very validated for her earlier assessment. "It could be."

Venus circled the large tank twice. Nothing. Funny how, when he'd mentioned the aquarium, something had eddied through her, a quick flash of something she couldn't get hold of. As usual. But now, when she was right here looking at the tank, there was nothing. No flashes, no odd feeling of déjà vu, nothing.

"When would you have time for them?" Venus asked, examining the huge tank that took up a good portion of the living room.

As long as it wasn't up to him to clean the tank— and it wasn't—the fish had no real claim to his schedule. "They're not like dogs, Venus. I don't have to take them out for a walk twice a day. Besides," he reminded her, "it's just temporary. My friend's gone to Europe for three months, not three years. It's his tank.

He just needed someone to take care of his fish until he got back."

She moved around the perimeter one last time, silently waiting for that the sliver of premonition she'd experienced when Trevor had first mentioned the aquarium.

"So he just dismantled the whole thing and brought it and the fish all here?"

It made more sense than she knew, he thought, given his penchant to get wrapped up in projects. "Easier than leaving them at his place—"

"Where you'd forget to feed them for a week," she guessed.

Trevor didn't even bother to deny it. Admittedly, he wasn't usually very good with details that didn't, on some level, somehow involve cooking.

"Give or take a few days," he allowed.

Venus hardly heard his answer. Unable to conjure up any familiar feelings, she was still mesmerized by what she saw. His absent friend had collected a great many exotic fish that seemed to get along.

"Look at them," she said softly. "Look at the way the light from the ceiling catches them." She bent over to get a little closer. "They are positively beautiful."

He watched her. Not the tank or the fish, but her. She was far more beautiful than the diverse squadron of fish milling around the tank. He had a feeling that she probably didn't think she was beautiful, but she was. Very. "If you say so," he murmured.

Something in his voice made her raise her eyes from

the tank. "You don't think all those multiple colors are beautiful?"

He didn't answer her directly. "I think the word *beautiful* should be used sparingly, applied as an adjective to something that really moves the soul."

Trevor was setting lofty bars, Venus thought. "Such as?"

"Such as a beautiful sunrise." And then, he added even more softly, "Or a beautiful woman."

The room around them seemed to grow very, very still. She could hear her own blood pumping through her veins. "I see."

"No," he corrected. "I see." Because he was looking directly at her, he added silently. "At the moment, you can't see. You can only remember."

He was hardly a measurable inch away from her now. Venus felt her breath get caught in her throat. Part of her was waiting for him to make another move, to say something that would take the burden of choice out of her hands.

But a part of her wanted to move forward. To make things happen rather than to simply mark time until they did. To grab hold of life before it was too late.

She had no idea where this sense of urgency came from. Whether it was because she was afraid that she would suddenly remember something that would separate her from this dear man. Or whether she was afraid that time was running out because, subconsciously, she was reacting to some kind of terminal situation. Or perhaps, in her other life, she'd been the type to let life happen to her. She didn't want to be a pawn, she wanted to be a player.

Turning from the tank, Venus slipped into the small

space that was created between the tank and Trevor, neatly confining her body in the less-than-ample pocket.

Mystified, Trevor could only look at her. "What are you doing?"

Her smile radiated from her eyes and filtered down to the curve of her mouth. She tilted her head back as she rose up on her toes.

"What does it look like I'm doing?"

He could feel her breath on his face as she spoke, could feel his gut tightening in response. "It looks like you're going to kiss me."

Amusement highlighted her features. "Very perceptive."

He was tempted, sorely tempted, but she didn't know if she was free to make this choice. If there wasn't someone waiting for her, worrying about her. "You sure you want to do this?"

The question wafted along her skin. Causing her to shiver. Not from the cold but from anticipation.

"Very sure," she whispered, wrapping her arms around his neck and sealing her body to his a moment before she did the same with her lips against his.

For a little thing she packed one hell of a punch, he caught himself thinking.

Damn but she made it tough to be honorable. Tough to do the right thing—especially when the only thing he wanted to do was kiss her until they were both senseless—and then make love with her.

The moment her lips touched his, he felt a series of explosions going off inside him, each one more powerful than the one before. Each one shaking him down to the core with progressively more impact. So much so that he thought he'd just splinter apart.

What was going on here?

Trevor couldn't remember ever feeling this alive and yet this needy, all at the same time. But if he crossed this line, if he gave in to the urges battering his body and made love with her, he knew there would be consequences to pay.

For him if not for her.

He'd never been like a lot of his peers, the ones who were satisfied with random, spontaneous couplings, done merely to savor the sensations and nothing more.

This most intimate of acts had a great deal of meaning for him.

It had never been about racking up mindless conquests, or about having sex just to feel that intoxicating rush. For him the rush came from having feelings for the woman he was making love with.

And never had he felt it as much as he did right at this moment.

But Trevor still wasn't able to shake the specter that hovered over him like an oppressive blanket. Couldn't shake the fear that he was about to do this, about to make love, with a married woman.

With what amounted to almost superhuman effort, Trevor struggled to separate himself from Venus. He held her at arm's length even though all he wanted to do was lose himself in her, in the scent of her, the promise of her.

He felt as if he were being ripped apart. "Venus, are you sure?"

Why was he doing this? Why was he trying to question her at a time like this?

From out of nowhere came the feeling that most men would have already had her clothes ripped off by now. Which made Trevor exceptionally kind, putting her needs before his own.

"I'm sure. I'll sign an affidavit to that effect if you want," she promised, her breath so short she was all but gasping.

She probably thought he was an idiot, Trevor thought. But he had more than his share of reasons—despite the fact that he also had a driving need to make love with her.

"I just don't want you to regret this in the morning."

"The only thing I'm going to regret in the morning is if I don't do this with you," she told him. A small sigh escaped her lips. "Trevor, I am actively throwing myself at you. The least you can do is have the decency to catch me."

"It's not the least," Trevor murmured against her mouth.

The next second, every single honorable intention he'd ever harbored left his body, swept away by a wave of desire the magnitude of which he'd never encountered before.

He wanted her so badly, he couldn't breathe.

On some distant plane, it occurred to him that this sensation rushing through him had all the ingredients of madness—or a heart attack. But hell, if he was going to go, he certainly couldn't think of a better way.

Caressing her curves, possessing her body from his very first touch, Trevor drew her away from the tank and the potential disaster. He wanted to be able to concentrate exclusively on her and not any crack that might occur to the tank.

The moment they were clear, he began peeling away her clothing, peeling away all the obstacles that stood between him and the flesh he was eager to touch, eager to savor. To make his own.

Her blouse slid off her shoulders, and then her arms, coaxed down by his eager, hot hands. His fingers tangled in her bra straps and it was all he could do not to rip them away. It wasn't easy, curbing his desire. Unsnapping the clasp on the bra took longer, but even that lent itself to building anticipation. It throbbed through his veins, growing more insistent.

The feel of her creamy skin against his palms was practically more than he could stand. He almost took her then and there before he managed, at the last moment, to rein himself in.

But romancing Venus, playing up her fantasies, was important. As important to him as he sensed it was to her. So he went as slowly as he was able, working her skirt and panties down along her hips. Doing it all with paced, deliberate movements.

His heart raced. As he pulled her naked, heated body to him, it took him a moment to realize his clothes had joined hers on the floor, wantonly scattered here and there. Whether by her design or his, he couldn't say. All he knew was that the clothes were gone and his body was on fire. The only thing that could put it out was the press of her body against his.

Or so he thought.

All that did was increase the urgency that roared like thunder through his veins. He wanted her that much more.

There was no turning back. Not for him. He prayed not for her because he didn't know what he would do if she suddenly asked him to stop.

Sliding his hands up and down her body, he found himself memorizing every dip, every curve, every perfect contour, all while kissing her over and over again. And very swiftly, they were both spent. And both ready to explode.

She felt reborn.

Although fairly certain that she wasn't a virgin, this was still all deliciously new to her. Venus let her instincts take over and found herself enthralled. Enthralled and completely in awe of what was going on. She couldn't have ever felt like this before.

She couldn't have, she silently insisted as he kissed the side of her neck and made a minisquadron of sensations go off like fireworks within her. She would have remembered this, remembered the man who had lit her up inside.

Yet, no man came to mind, no fireworks display was recreated. This was all original, all being felt and richly savored for the first time.

Somehow, it seemed fitting. He'd rescued her, caused her to live again. It was fitting that she become his.

Just when she thought she'd experienced all there was, she discovered that there was more.

So much more.

The fireworks were no longer in her head, they were in every part of her body.

She sensed it was all coming to one grand crescendo. Eager to experience it all, Venus lifted her hips up to his in a silent invitation.

Trevor finally drove himself into her. The next moment, she closed her legs around his lower torso, drawing him into her as far as she could just as the final explosion occurred.

It was worth the buildup, she remembered thinking just before her mind separated itself from her body and floated away.

Chapter Eleven

For a moment, he thought of quietly slipping back into the restaurant and letting Venus have her privacy.

It was a night very much like when he'd rescued her. Maybe that was why she'd been drawn here to the terrace. She was leaning against the railing and staring at the ocean.

He found himself watching her for another moment, wondering what she was thinking.

Wondering about her.

He no longer cared about the woman she'd been. He only knew that he was attracted to the woman she was. The woman who steadily crept into his heart.

The restaurant had closed its doors for the night forty minutes ago. Twenty minutes ago, the last of the patrons had walked out of the restaurant, silver foil swans filled with leftovers clutched in their hands. Shortly thereafter, the rest of his staff had gone home for the night.

All except for Venus.

But when he looked for her in order to take her home, she was nowhere to be found. When he called her, there was no answer. From out of nowhere, panic sliced through him, lethal and sharp.

What if she was gone?

What if she'd suddenly remembered who she was and, overwhelmed, had rushed out to rejoin her life without saying goodbye?

That was crazy, he upbraided himself. Venus would never do that. She would have said something to him before leaving.

But then, he'd never been this happy before, or this excited about a relationship. It was only natural to assume that such happiness didn't exist in the real world. So he went looking for her when he should have been busy shutting the rest of the restaurant down. When he found her, the sense of relief was amazing. That was when he knew he was in trouble. He was getting too close—but he couldn't seem to help himself.

The breeze played with her hair, ruffling it with cool affection. He walked up quietly behind her, still debating whether or not to disturb her. Just as he made his decision to withdraw again and turn away, he heard her voice, soft, low, ask, "Who do you think I was?"

Trevor crossed the terrace again and slipped his arms around her waist, standing behind her. He held Venus to him, thinking how natural this all felt. As if this was where his life was supposed to be, right here, in this spot, with this woman.

"You mean before I pulled you out of the water?"

He heard Venus sigh. In frustration? Resignation? He couldn't tell. And her response gave him no clue. "Yes."

"That's easy." He felt her turn her head against his chest, her eyes raised in silent surprise. "A mermaid. A wondrous, mythical creature too beautiful to exist in the real world—except that you did. And do."

She turned completely around to look up at him, her breasts brushing against his chest, sending shockwaves of warmth through him. Any sort of physical contact with her, however minor, always did that these days. It was hard to imagine that only two months had gone by since he'd saved her. It felt like a lifetime.

It felt like a blink of an eye.

"No, really," she pressed. "It's been almost nine weeks since you found me. Shouldn't I be remembering something? My name, or who I was, where I came from? Just some tidbit."

Trevor could feel her frustration. Empathy surged through him. He knew how he'd feel in her place—like a prisoner.

"I don't know." He leaned his cheek against the top of her head, drawing in the scent of her hair. Savoring it. "I just know that I'm lucky to have found you and that if you remember, then maybe I'll lose you. So, to be honest, I'm not all that eager to try to figure out who you were." She drew back her head to look at him. "I only know that I really, really like who you are."

Venus smiled then and threaded her arms around his neck, curving her body into his. "Me, too. I was just thinking that if I never remember anything about my past, maybe that wouldn't be so bad. I'm happy. From what I hear, that's not such an easy thing." Her eyes shone as they looked up into his. "I like being happy with you."

His heart felt so full, he thought it would burst. This was a very new sensation for him. Even when he'd been with Alicia, he hadn't felt like this. He hesitated to name the feeling. For now, he was just going to savor what was.

Trevor held her close to him. Held her so close that there was no space for negative thoughts. The kind of thoughts that played devil's advocate and whispered in his mind. There was no denying that he felt as if he were on borrowed time. No denying that he was falling for this mermaid he'd pulled from the sea. Because any plans for a future with her could only be laid on a foundation of sand, he forced himself to focus only on the moment.

Even if it meant that he was functioning in a fool's paradise.

So he stood there with Venus in his arms, saying nothing, living in the moment, grateful that it was there.

The banner across the front of Kate's Kitchen proclaimed it to be closed for a private party. It didn't mention that the private party was his brother and new sister-in-law's wedding reception.

For the last week and a half, Trevor had pulled double duty and made preparations for the celebration while still running his restaurant at maximum perfection. Sleep became a rarity.

To his pleasant surprise, Venus had been invaluable. She was there with him every step of the way, acting both as his right hand and his gofer, doing whatever was needed. It amazed him at how tirelessly she worked with him and how well they meshed together. And every minute of every day, as they worked, he thought about turning their partnership into a permanent thing.

But there was no time to talk about anything except the reception. The time beyond that seemed far away. Trevor tried to convince himself that this was a blessing.

And then, finally, the day of the wedding came. His mind was on last-minute preparations. For him, the ceremony was a blur. All except for how beautiful Venus looked in an electric-blue gown that defied gravity and emphasized her small waist.

As beautiful as the gown was, he longed to see her without it. The thought kept him going long after his energy should have been depleted.

"Trevor, you outdid yourself," Kate said, finding him an hour into the reception. As if to emphasize her sentiment, the seven-tier wedding cake was brought out and housed in a corner until later. It looked more like a work of art than something spun out of flour, eggs and sugar.

As ever, Trevor received the compliments with modesty. "I had help." Looking around, he saw Venus bringing a bottle of champagne to the table that Travis and Trent, along with their dates, shared. He beckoned her over. "I'm not sure if I could have pulled it off without Venus."

Venus joined him just in time to hear the second part of his statement.

"You would have." There was no false modesty to her words. She meant them. "All I did was run some errands and pick up some of the slack. It's your menu, your recipes, your show," she added. "Can I get you anything, Mrs. Marlowe?"

"No, and it's Kate, please," she reminded the younger woman. Kate placed a hand on each of their shoulders. "You both did a great job," she complimented them with sincerity, then added a bit more softly, "You make a nice team."

Trevor laughed, shaking his head. "There you go again, Mom, being subtle."

Kate looked from her son to the woman she thought perfectly suited to him. "I think we're possibly past that at this point. In fact, I'm sure of it. Why don't you two go and dance a little?" she suggested, then bent down, lowering her voice. Her next words were for Venus's benefit. "I taught him how to dance so he has no excuse."

That might be the case with Trevor, Venus thought, but there was another possible obstacle. "I'm afraid I don't know if *I* know how to dance."

Emilio was handling the kitchen, along with several of the staff he had retained for tonight. That left him as free as he chose to be.

Trevor never hesitated. He extended his hand to Venus. "Why don't we go and find out?"

Gamely, she slipped her hand into his. "Okay, but if I step all over you," she warned, "remember, you asked for it."

He made his way over to the dance floor. "That

doesn't exactly make me shake in my shoes. Being stepped on by someone who weighs maybe a hundred pounds if she fills her pockets with rocks doesn't hold much terror for me."

"I weigh more than that," she protested.

"With the rocks in your pockets?" he asked, drawing her into his arms. It was a slow song and he began to sway to the rhythm.

Without realizing it, she fell into step, her movements echoing his. "No, seriously, I weigh…" And then her voice trailed off. She raised her eyes to his face, frustration and wonder mirrored there. "I don't know how much I weigh."

Trevor bent his head down so that his words were only heard by her. "My guess about your weight would be that it's perfect."

She could feel herself smiling inside. "You are very good for my ego."

"Anytime," he murmured. "Oh, and by the way, you can dance."

She'd forgotten about that. After checking her foot placement, she then glanced up at him, more than a little satisfaction and pleasure warming her. "I guess I can."

She did more than just go through the motions, shadowing him. Venus could feel the rhythm throbbing through her, could feel the beat from her fingertips all the way down to her feet. Was this a natural ability? Or had someone taught her?

Small questions nagged her but the urgency to know the answer diminished with each passing day.

"They really look happy together, don't they?" Trevor

commented. When she raised her head, he nodded his toward Mike and Miranda.

As she looked in their direction, something small and troubling reared its head. She couldn't put her finger on it, couldn't explain it. It was like the sudden appearance of a pebble in her shoe. A splintered thought flashed in her brain, a hairsbreadth away from taking on form.

And then, the next moment, it was gone. Disappearing into vapor.

Mentally, she shrugged it off. She nodded in response to Trevor's question. "Yes, they do."

"Would you be happy…?" he asked her. "Married," he added.

Oh God, this was coming out all wrong, Trevor rebuked himself. He was so much better at creating things in the kitchen than stringing the right words together. She probably thought he was some kind of mentally arrested idiot.

"I don't know," she told him. All of a sudden, her stomach ached, the sides pinching together at the very mention of the idea. But because an answer seemed important to Trevor, she pushed on. "I do know that it would depend on who I was marrying."

"How about me?" That, too, didn't come out right, he thought, but he'd given up trying to wax poetic. The main thing was to get the words out.

Stunned, she stopped dancing. "How about you what?"

He took a deep breath, then plunged into the icy waters. "Marriage. How about if I was the one you were marrying?"

For a moment, she said nothing. She forced herself to

push back the wall of fear that threatened to overwhelm her. She had no idea what had generated it, only that fear had no right to be in the same place that Trevor occupied.

"Then yes," she answered, "I would be happy."

The song ended just then and people returned to their tables. He took her hand in his. Instead of returning to their table, Trevor led her to the terrace. He closed the doors behind them.

The night air was chilly and she wrapped her arms around herself as she waited for him to speak.

"Do you want my jacket?" he offered.

"No, I'm okay. Did you want to say something to me in private?" she guessed.

Trevor slipped his hand into his pants pocket. His fingers curled around something small and square. It was still there. The box he'd placed there this morning after he'd gotten dressed for the wedding. The box he'd gotten at the jeweler's when he picked up Mike and Miranda's wedding rings.

Taking it out of his pocket, he slipped it into her hand and closed her fingers over it.

She looked down at her hand. Her heart slammed against her rib cage. There was hardly enough air in her lungs to ask, "What's this?"

Nerves tangled around uncertainty. "Why don't you open it and see?"

Whatever air she did have in her lungs came to a complete standstill, as did everything else, freezing in place as she opened the box.

A feeling of déjà vu washed over her.

She'd done this before, been in this exact same place once before, looking down at an engagement ring.

She waited. Nothing else materialized, no insight, no faces, no breakthrough. Nothing.

But the feeling of elation that came rushing at her, that was new. That was different. She would have sworn to it on a stack of Bibles.

"It's beautiful." Venus raised her eyes to his, almost afraid to ask, afraid of spoiling the moment. "Are you asking me to marry you?"

"In my own, inept, clumsy way, yes. Yes, I am." Taking the ring out of the box, Trevor slipped it on her finger. "I know it's only been a short while, but I feel as if I've known you forever. I can't really remember what my life was like without you."

She grinned from ear to ear. She couldn't help it. What she felt inside came spilling out. "That makes two of us. Except that in my case, Trevor, it's actually true."

He took her into his arms. "In my case, too," he whispered just before he kissed her.

Despite the happiness in the foreground, something bothered her. Some nagging little detail that refused to take on shape or dimension. But this time, she didn't even try to make it clearer. Instead, she shut the fragments out, refused to try to put them together. All she wanted was to savor the moment and the man.

Venus molded her body to his, absorbing the kiss and every wave of heat that went with it. The happiness she felt was real and that was all—*all*—that mattered, she silently insisted.

I love you, Trevor Marlowe, with every inch of my body and soul. I always will, she silently swore even as the kiss took her deeper and deeper into a deliciously endless abyss.

The sound of a distant, delicate cough penetrated. Reluctantly, Venus drew back, letting the world back in. Kate was sharing the terrace with them, standing just at the door.

"Hey, you two, sorry to interrupt, but Miranda's about the throw the bouquet," she told them, beckoning them both inside.

"I don't need a bouquet," Venus said. To prove it, she held up her hand in the classic pose of newly engaged women everywhere: wrist bent to show the ring off to its maximum advantage.

Moonlight reflected off the surface of the pear-shaped diamond, making it appear blindingly brilliant.

Kate made no effort to hide her pleasure, pleasure that came with only the smallest drop of surprise. She threw her arms open and embraced not her son, but the woman who had captured his heart.

"Welcome to the family, Venus," she cried.

"Hey, what about me?" Trevor asked. Theirs was a demonstrative family, thanks to Kate. "Don't I get a hug, too?"

The smile on Kate's lips made her look like the personification of mischief. "I'll let Venus take care of that." Stepping back, she eased the door closed. "Carry on" was her parting whisper.

Wiggling her hand just a little, Venus watched in rapt fascination as the light from the lamp on the table played off the stone on her finger, catching it and breaking it apart into a hundred separate, dazzling colors.

Trevor slid down beside her on his sofa. Rather than take her back to his parents' house after the reception, he'd brought her to his apartment for a private celebration.

"I'll buy you a bigger one when I can afford it," he promised. He had been tempted to get a much larger stone to begin with, but a large debt was not the way to begin a new life together.

"Don't you dare," she cried, covering her ring protectively with her other hand. "I don't want a bigger stone, I want this one."

"Most women like big stones." He wasn't an expert on women by a long shot, but that seemed to be the way things were.

"That's when it's a bribe because they're not getting a man of quality." The moment the words were out of her mouth, she felt her stomach pinch again, as if she'd uncovered a deeper awareness. But this wasn't about her, this was about *them*. "I would have taken a string of yarn tied in a bow as long as you came with it."

"I can afford more than a string of yarn," he told her with a laugh. "And judging from the way you've been looking at the stone, I don't think yarn would have had the same impact."

"I'm just appreciating what it stands for." She raised her eyes to his. "Are you sure you want to marry me, Trevor?" The last thing she wanted to do was to scare him off, but he had a right to know the chance he was taking. "You don't know what you're getting. For all you know, I could be a convicted felon on the run, or a serial killer who went off the deep end because of all the murders she's committed. Neither one of us knows who I really am."

She was adorable when she was trying to be serious, he thought, doing his best not to laugh out loud. "Mom told me that they took your fingerprints at the police station. If you'd turned up in the database, we would have heard by now. You're not a felon."

She accepted that—sort of. "Maybe I'm a clever con artist."

Completely adorable, he underscored. "And you're what? After me for my cookware?"

"Hey, you've got some pretty snazzy pots at the restaurant," she deadpanned.

"Now I know what to buy you for Christmas." Growing serious, he looked at her for a long moment. "You know I love you, don't you?"

"I kind of figured that out when you gave me the ring." The smile on her lips rose into her eyes. "I love you, too."

He didn't say anything in response. Instead, he picked her up into his arms and carried her to his bedroom. Trevor had always been a firm believer that actions spoke louder than words.

Chapter Twelve

No rest for the wicked, Venus thought.

But then, she really didn't want any. Not tonight. She spent the rest of the night either making love with Trevor, or resting after the fact, curled up against him and feeling incredibly content.

Each time one of them began to doze off, the other would wind up arousing them either through a caress, or a tender kiss innocently planted on a cheek, a forehead or the top of a head.

It took very little to set either one of them off. She should have been exhausted. Instead, she was thrilled and raring to go with very little encouragement.

Maybe it had to do with the wedding they'd attended, or the proposal that had arisen from it. Whatever the reason, they couldn't seem to get enough of one another tonight.

In the beginning, Venus thought it was only her, because she was experiencing something singularly wonderful. But after the second time, as she paused to regroup, she realized that it was the same for Trevor. Not ten minutes after they'd reached the highest peak, he was lightly outlining her ear with his tongue, sending waves of hot shivers down her spine, magically renewing her energy levels.

Twisting, Venus turned into him, moving so that her body wound up on top of his. From her vantage point, she smiled down into his face. "I don't remember ever being this happy."

"Said the woman whose memory only goes back for a total of seventy-three days."

That he remembered the number of days touched her deeply. She wondered if all men were that thoughtful, that caring. "My memory might not go back any further than that, but there's this feeling I have—"

Her weight hardly pinned him down, but all he raised was his head to look at her. "Yes?"

"This feeling that I've never been this happy, never felt this good before." For a moment, she folded her hands on his chest and rested her chin there, her eyes on his. "I can't really explain it, it's just something I feel in my bones. A 'given' for lack of a better term." She paused, searching for the right words. "And it makes me afraid."

His eyes narrowed as he tried to follow her train of thought. "Afraid?"

She nodded, the ends of her red hair moving ever so softly along his bare chest, tickling him. "Afraid that I'm too happy. Isn't there supposed to be some kind of balance in the universe? A yin followed by a yang?"

It amazed him the things she remembered when she couldn't remember her own name. "Maybe this is the 'yang.' Maybe you've already had the 'yin.'"

That didn't seem right to her. "But—"

He threw her a curveball. "You're almost perfect, you know."

Her mood switching to playful, Venus decided to rise to the bait. "Almost?"

He nodded. "But sometimes, you think too much. Talk too much."

Before she had a chance to refute his statement or defend herself, Trevor framed her face with his hands and brought his mouth up to hers, kissing her hard. Melting away her concerns until all that was left was an overwhelming desire to become one with him again. To make love with him until they reached utter exhaustion.

"You know—" her words came in short spurts, her lungs rapidly depleting their air supply "—I think we're setting some kind of a record here."

He paused for a moment, cupping her cheek. "In order to get into the *Guinness Book of World Records,* there has to be a third, disinterested party keeping tally." Brushing a kiss against her lips, he laughed softly. "I doubt anyone seeing you like this could remain disinterested for more than five seconds." He reconsidered the assessment. "Less."

Raising her head, she shook it, sending her hair flying like a curtain of fire. "I don't want a third party, disinterested or otherwise, anywhere near us when we make love."

His laugh filled the apartment. "Why, Venus, you're shy."

She lowered her head again, her face inches from his. When she spoke, her lips all but brushed against his. "Now who's talking too much?"

He felt his gut tightening. What was it about this woman that made him want her so? "You're absolutely right. Why am I talking when my mouth could be doing something far more rewarding?"

And with that, his lips began to move down along the smooth expanse of her throat, working their way down her breasts, leaving reignited flames in their wake. Venus made no effort to conceal how crazy he made her. She twisted and turned against him, absorbing the sensations he created within her.

The evening continued. They continued. She lost track of how many times they wound up making love, lost track of everything except the happiness that was all but exploding in her veins, even hours after they drifted into a semisleep in each other's arms.

The sound of stealthlike movement registered in some far-away region of her brain, which seemed to fall into gear long before the rest of her did. With great reluctance, she pried her eyes open.

She lay facedown on a pillow. Daylight pushed its way into Trevor's bedroom, reaching the corners and painting them gold. Turning her head toward the sound, Venus blinked twice before focusing on the figure on the far side of the room.

Trevor.

He was hunting for socks in the bureau.

"You're up," she murmured. "And dressed."

The sound of her voice drew a rueful smile from him as he looked in her direction. "I'm sorry, I tried not to wake you."

Unless he was sneaking off to see another woman, she couldn't see why he shouldn't wake her. Exhaustion had finally caught up with her. She gave herself two more minutes.

"What time is it?"

"Nine."

That did it for her. Any thoughts of lingering evaporated. Venus bolted upright. "Nine? Aren't we supposed to be at work?"

He tried not to notice that she was sitting up in bed, nude except for the sheet pooling around her hips. Trevor could feel his blood heating again. Instantly. He wouldn't have thought that possible, not after the night they had just shared. He was surprised he had any energy left to react.

But he obviously did because he wanted to pull the sheet from her, wanted to shed the clothes he'd just put on and make love to her slowly, with precision instead of just heat.

Trevor forced himself to study the headboard behind her back. "Go back to sleep, Venus. You can have the day off."

Rather than please her, favoritism bothered her. Was that something about her character? Or was that part of the new person she was? "You're not taking the day off," she pointed out. No one took a day off and then wore a tie.

"I'm the boss."

She inclined her head. "And I'm not supposed to get preferential treatment," she reminded him.

She didn't want the staff at Kate's Kitchen to think that she was sleeping with the boss to get ahead. She liked the people she worked with and they seemed to like her. Venus didn't want anything getting in the way of that.

Trevor laughed, crossing back to the bed. He stole a quick kiss. "Too late for that. Unless you think what went on last night happens between me and all my employees."

She grinned. She trusted him. Without being told, she knew in her heart that Trevor wouldn't cheat on her, wouldn't take advantage of any woman who worked with him. "I wouldn't have thought that Emilio was your type," she deadpanned.

He tossed a pillow at her. "If you're not going back to sleep, wise guy, put something on before I forget all my newly formed good intentions and go back to having my way with you."

She grinned. "Certainly don't know your way around a proper threat, do you?" If anything, his words made her want to goad him on. Tucking the sheet around herself, she slid to the edge of the bed. "I'm going to have to stop at your parents' house for a change of clothes. I don't think a strapless evening gown is the proper outfit to wear under an apron."

"Right now," he said, catching her in his arms and dragging her up to her feet, savoring the feel of her body, "I'd like to see you wearing nothing beneath the apron but an inviting smile."

Venus laughed, draping her arms around his neck. "That can be arranged," she told him, mischief gleaming in her eyes. "Tonight." She whispered the last word like a seductive promise.

She'd certainly blossomed these last two months, he couldn't help thinking. Her transformation had gone from her being an uncertain young woman to one who grabbed on to the life she had with both hands.

And she'd caused a change to come about in him, as well. She'd broadened his life, made him think beyond menus and profitable quarters. He still worked hard, still aimed for success, but now there was a bigger reason. Now he wanted to do it for her.

For them.

He wanted, more than anything, to make certain there was a future waiting for them—and the family to come. He might have rescued her from the sea, but she had certainly rescued him from the narrow world in which he'd unconsciously imprisoned himself.

"It's a date," he whispered back, brushing his lips against hers quickly.

He fought the temptation to make love to her again. But if he gave in, if he allowed himself even the most fleeting taste of her lips, it would only lead to another. And another. And they both knew where that led.

Taking her hand, he gently pulled Venus out of the bed.

Then, instead of letting go, he looked down at her hand. Specifically at the third finger. His mouth curved in satisfaction.

"Looks like it's still there," he murmured, raising his eyes to hers.

What an odd thing to say, she thought. "Did you think I'd lose it?"

"No, I was just afraid that I'd imagined the whole thing. That you didn't say yes."

"I still don't know me very well," she confessed, "but I'm fairly certain I'm not stupid. And letting someone like you slip away would be one of the stupidest things a person could do."

"Saying no to me would be the height of stupidity."

The strange, disembodied male voice rose out of nowhere and echoed in her head. For a moment, she was afraid she was hallucinating. And then she became aware of Trevor's arms around her. A feeling of well-being pervaded through her, blocking out the effect generated by the voice.

Trevor looked at her, concerned. She'd gone pale again. "What's the matter?" he asked. "Did you remember something?"

"No..." She shook her head. Rather than try to replay the voice in her head, she deliberately blocked it. "It was just that annoying feeling of déjà vu, here for a second, then gone again."

Instinct guided her. She didn't want to explore where the voice had come from, or who it belonged to, afraid that the answers might undo her. Undo her new world.

She'd crossed a line recently, no longer wanting to know who she'd been before. Only wanting to savor who she was now. Trevor's fiancée.

Venus glanced at the dress on the floor. The dress he had peeled off her so slowly last night, she thought she'd explode, consumed by desire, before he finally got it off her. "Um, won't your parents say something about my being in the same outfit as yesterday?"

He grinned. At times she was wonderfully innocent. He liked the fact that she cared about what his parents thought of her. He liked everything about her.

He kissed her forehead with deep affection. "I think by now they've noticed that you didn't come home last night and they've put two and two together."

A smile played on her lips. A glimmer of mischief entered her eyes. "More like one and one."

Bending down, Trevor picked up the dress and handed it to her with more than a trace of reluctance. "Don't tempt me, Venus. I'm already running late."

Venus let the dress he'd handed her slip through her fingers back down to the floor. Shedding the sheet that still clung to her, she stepped forward and pressed her nude body against his, causing delicious sensations to race through her. Anticipation had brought them up to yet another, higher plateau.

The smile on her lips and in her eyes was seduction itself. "Well, since you're already running late, what's another few minutes?"

Oh, the hell with it, he thought. He didn't have to get in early. They didn't open until eleven-thirty. Emilio knew what to do and had said more than once he'd be willing to jump in if needed.

"A few minutes?" he echoed, taking her face between his hands.

His heart swelled. She'd breeched an area that he thought would never be touched again. When his mother had died in the plane crash, he had been the most devastated. Out of the four of them, he had been the one who'd withdrawn the most, grieved the hardest. Felt abandoned. His heart had frozen in self-defense. Kate had done her best, but there was always a part of him that had been held in reserve, a part of him that refused to become involved.

That part was gone now, merged with the rest of him. He loved this woman completely and utterly to the bottom of his soul. And though she had said yes to him, his vulnerability worried him even though he could no longer do anything about it.

"Are you telling me that I'm too fast?"

"No," she breathed. "You're just right." Her eyes shone as she told him how she felt. "You're the perfect lover."

"You," he informed her, kissing her once, then twice, and then again, heating more with each pass of his mouth, "have nothing to compare it to."

She twined her arms around his neck, bending into him, into the wonder that his mouth created all through her. She would have thought this was their first time. Instead of the best time, she amended silently, because that was what it seemed like. Each time was better than the last. Improving on perfection.

"Don't have to," she asserted. "Some things you just know. Some things fall into the realm of absolute."

She seemed so serious, he would have laughed if it wouldn't have hurt her feelings. God, but he wanted her. Forever and always. "Is that so?"

"That's so." Pulling back after more passionate kisses, she pretended to frown slightly. "Am I going to have to rip your clothes off your body, or are you going to get naked voluntarily?"

"Voluntarily." Trevor chuckled as he loosened his tie.

But Venus shook her head. "Too slow," she declared. To make her point, she yanked his tie off the rest of the way, tossing it on the floor. Her eyes never left his. What he saw there quickened his gut. The next moment, she was pushing his jacket off his shoulders and down his arms. Even the sound of her breathing, audible and shallow, had his pulse accelerating.

"Nothing like a shy, retiring woman to turn me on," he told her.

She stopped suddenly, raising her eyes to his. Questions shot out of nowhere, filling her head. "Have there been many? Before me," she clarified, then strung the words together to make more sense. "Have there been many women in your life before me?"

He pulled his arms free of the jacket, and the shirt she'd unbuttoned simultaneously, sending them to the floor in a heap. As he tilted her head back with his hand, his mouth captured hers again. The kiss was deep and seemingly endless.

"None that I can remember," he told her honestly when he finally drew back just a little.

And it was true. The women he'd been with, the ones he'd taken to his bed in hopes of getting close to, in hopes of actually *feeling* something for, just blended together in his head, one patchwork quilt of faces all merging into one.

No one stood out in his mind but her.

"Not even Alicia?"

"Not even Alicia," he replied.

Her mouth curved against his just before she returned to the kiss. "Nice to know."

It took them another forty-five minutes before they finally made it out the door, temporarily sated. And then another half hour to reach his parents' house.

It would have been faster, but Murphy's Law had gone into effect and there had been an accident on the road, a truck versus an SUV. Police cars, ambulances and fire trucks had all been summoned to the scene, all doing their share to impede the flow of traffic. Rather than flow, the traffic didn't even trickle. As a result, everything came to a near standstill and he was too embroiled to take an alternate route.

"We're really going to be late," Venus commented, worried.

He spared her a glance. "I don't regret a second of it."

The smile he saw cross her lips made everything worth it.

As Trevor finally turned onto the cul de sac where his parents' house was located, he automatically glanced toward their driveway to see if someone was home. From the look of it, everyone was home. His mother, his father and his sister.

And someone else.

He didn't recognize the sleek white Ford Crown Victoria parked at the curb directly in front of his parents' house, but it occurred to him that the police department favored that make and model for its officers and detectives.

What was it doing here?

The potential answer did nothing to reassure him.

Suddenly, all the happiness that had filled him just a moment ago evaporated, pushed aside by a wall of anxiety.

Whoever had come was here about Venus.

Chapter Thirteen

Trevor's first instinct was to make a wide U-turn, turn the car around and head back to his apartment. But running would only postpone the inevitable.

If there was an inevitable.

After all, it might not be what he thought. He might just be overreacting, dramatizing it in his head because he was so afraid of losing the happiness he'd stumbled across.

So afraid of losing her.

Maybe the owner of the Crown Victoria car had parked it at the curb in front of his parents' house because there were no other available spaces. With ten houses packed into the cul de sac and each residence having at least two cars if not more, parking on the block was at a premium.

The white vehicle didn't necessarily *have* to belong to

a member of the police department, Trevor argued silently. Other people drove white Crown Victorias besides law enforcement agents.

Trevor's heart felt like lead in his chest.

He was only fooling himself. He didn't believe in coincidences. With the car parked right here, after they'd gone to the police station, only one explanation made sense. A potential match to Venus had been found.

Venus sensed it, too. He could tell by her body language. Looking out the window, she had become ramrod-stiff in her seat.

Trevor tried his best to sound upbeat, as if this could only be a good thing. And, after all, just because someone might claim her didn't mean she was married. It could be a mother, father, sister, brother or even a second aunt, twice removed, who had come for her.

So why did he feel like a prisoner walking the last mile?

"Looks like we're about to find out your secret identity, Venus," he said with all the cheerfulness that he could muster.

She surprised him by putting her hand on his arm, squeezing hard. It was an urgent gesture. "Drive," she told him.

It was the last thing he'd expected to hear from her. "What?"

"Drive," she repeated, more urgently this time. "Go to the restaurant. Go back to your apartment. Anyplace. Just drive."

He wanted to. God help him, he wanted to. But if he did, if somehow they managed to elude whatever or whoever was waiting for her in his parents' house, it would only be temporary. And until they knew what it was, she would always wonder what had been waiting for her behind door number one.

So he took the lead, telling himself he had to be strong. For both their sakes. "Venus, I really doubt that the police detective you spoke to at the precinct is here on a social call or because he's hoping to get an early-bird discount at Kate's Kitchen."

Venus dropped her hand from his arm, letting it fall into her lap. Her eyes were downcast. "I know," she said so quietly he had to strain to hear her. "That's why I want you to drive away."

Did she know something? Had something come back to her? Was she afraid? "Don't you want to find out who you are?"

"No." She turned to him, her eyes asking him not to do this, not to make her go in. "No, I don't," she emphasized. "I like where I'm at right now. I like who I am." She took a breath. "Maybe I won't after I find out."

"Whatever your name is, Venus, Jane or Rumplestiltskin, it doesn't matter." He waved away any possible label. "You're still you inside."

She blew out a long breath. "Right now, the 'me' inside is really scared, Trevor. Really scared," she repeated softly, glancing toward the front door.

"There's nothing to be scared of." For a second, he laced his hand through hers, affording her the strength of human contact. "I'll be there with you all the way."

He was wrong, she thought. There *was* something to

be scared of. The minute she walked in through that door, she stood to lose everything. She could feel it.

"There's everything to be scared of," she countered. "What if I'm married?"

It was the same question that haunted him. He strove to be the voice of reason, despite the fact that he felt anything but reasonable. "Wouldn't you rather know than not know?"

"No." She shook her head so hard, her hair fairly bounced along. "There's a reason they say no news is good news." The jitteriness inside her continued to grow. "Because until you get that news, you can go on pretending that everything's okay. Once you hear it, there's no more pretending."

Trevor slipped his arm around her as best he could and pulled her to him. Inclining his head, he kissed her.

"Everything *is* going to be okay," he said with such certainty that she was tempted to believe him. Though she knew he had no power to make such a guarantee, she clung to his words as if they were a talisman that could protect her.

"I'll hold you to that," she whispered against his chest.

He threaded his fingers through her hair, loving the earthy, soft feel. "Deal." Drawing back, he unbuckled his seat belt. "Ready?"

She took a deep breath. The butterflies in her stomach refused to calm down. "Ready."

After getting out of the vehicle, he came around to her side and opened the door for her. When he took her hand in his, it felt icy. He made no comment, only gave her a squeeze and smiled as encouragingly as he could at her.

The moment they walked into the house, Trevor's heart sank.

His parents were in the living room, sitting on the sofa. Both were dressed for work and ready to go at a moment's notice. Opposite them, on the love seat, was a rumpled-looking man with faded chestnut hair. He appeared as if he'd inhabited his skin a very long time and the fit was not always a good one. The other man was his complete antithesis. He was younger, handsome, impeccably groomed and had an air about him that fairly shouted of affluence, confidence and success.

Seeing them, the younger man rose to his feet like someone in a trance. And then he crossed to them—to her—in less than a heartbeat.

"Oh God, I thought you were dead, Gemma," he cried, embracing her. Venus stood there, her arms pinned to her sides, a look of dismay and surprise on her face. She didn't know this man.

Trevor wanted to pull her away, to offer her the shelter of his own arms. But he held himself in check, even though a wave of hostility rose inside him.

If this was supposedly someone of significance in her life, where the hell had he been for the last two months? Biding his time? Waiting for her to show up on her own? Damn, if he'd been the one who'd lost Venus, he would have moved heaven and earth and all the locations in between until he'd found her.

Venus withstood the man's embrace as long as she felt it politely necessary, then drew back and away from the stranger who smelled of rich cologne. "Who's Gemma?" she asked.

A frown marred almost perfect features. "You're

kidding, right?" He eyed her incredulously, as if waiting for a punch line.

"She's not kidding," Trevor informed him tersely. He didn't add what he desperately wanted to say: back off.

He looked at his parents, as if to ask why they even had this man here in their house.

"We told you that she had amnesia," Bryan reminded the young man.

The man's eyes shifted from Venus, back to Bryan. "I know that's what you said, but I really didn't believe it," he admitted. The expression on his face was just slightly rueful. "I guess I should have." He examined the others like a man accustomed to getting answers when he posed questions. "How long is something like this supposed to last?"

"There's no telling," Trevor informed him, barely curbing his dislike. Something about the man rubbed him the wrong way. "The doctor in the E.R. said that it might come back all at once—or not at all," he added with significant weight.

The response left the other man unfazed. "It'll come back," he said confidently. "I've just got to get her home, in familiar surroundings. We were supposed to get married the Sunday she disappeared," he explained, never realizing that he'd just cut out Trevor's heart. "I thought she'd accidentally fallen overboard and drowned, like that actress did years ago. Natalie somebody-or-other."

"Wood," Kate interjected softly. "You're referring to Natalie Wood."

"Whatever," the young man muttered irreverently.

Trevor didn't care for his response to his mother,

either. This guy was a developmentally arrested human being, he thought.

"But all that doesn't matter," the younger man was saying, addressing his words to a distressed Venus. "You're alive and you're safe." He continued holding her hand as if she were his property and had no right to freedom without his say-so. "The marriage license is still good for another three weeks. Why don't we just go to city hall and get married right now?" he suggested like someone who expected not to be crossed. "I've got a friend who's a judge."

Whoa, what was he trying to pull? "What's your hurry?" Trevor asked.

The man's expression clearly said that he had no right to question him. "No hurry. By my calculations, even though it's no business of yours, we're two months late."

Out of the corner of his eye, he saw both his mother's and his father's annoyance. "And where have you been those two months?" Trevor inquired. "We filed a report about her the morning of the day after I pulled her out of the ocean."

Instead of answering, the man turned to Venus. "Then you did fall overboard."

"Apparently," Venus murmured. Something withdrew inside her, curling up into a little ball. Had she really been engaged to marry this man? He was too sleek, too picture-perfect and, if her instincts were right, too in love with the sound of his own voice to be someone she would care for enough to marry.

And yet, why would he go to the trouble of looking for her and showing up to take her with him if it was all a lie? The answer was, he wouldn't. That meant that they were engaged.

A shiver slithered up and down her spine.

"My God, what a terrible ordeal you've been through," he said, implying that life with the Marlowes was a "terrible ordeal." "But all that's behind you. I'm here now and I'm going to take care of you."

"She doesn't need anyone to take care of her," Trevor fairly growled. He hardly recognized his own voice and saw Kate looking at him in surprise. "She can take care of herself."

The man scowled at him. "And you are?"

Trevor squelched the overwhelming desire to say, "None of your business" and instead answered civilly, "Trevor Marlowe."

"Well, Trevor Marlowe—" the other man enunciated his name with an ill-concealed air of haughtiness "—I've known Gemma for six years. And you've known her for, what, a couple of months perhaps?" There was contempt in his eyes. "That hardly qualifies you as an expert on what she needs or doesn't need."

Until that moment, Trevor hadn't known he had a temper, but he felt it flaring. Keeping his anger under control took considerable effort. "Something tells me that when it comes to Venus—"

The man wore an expression of disgust, as if he'd just discovered a dead rat inside his shoe. "And just who is this Venus?"

Venus raised her chin and proclaimed with quiet dignity, "I am."

The man in the expensive suit appeared to tap in to what could only be assumed as a very short supply of patience and answered, "No, you're Gemma Burnett, daughter of the late Hayden Burnett, and I'm Baylor Evans—" he took her hand in his and raised it to his lips, pressing a kiss to her knuckles "—your fiancé and your father's successor at Richfield Bank."

Venus pulled back her hand just as Bryan asked, "The international banking firm?"

Maybe his eyes were playing tricks on him, but from where Trevor was standing, it looked as if the man who'd just nibbled Venus's knuckles puffed up his chest.

"The very same. Apparently someone here actually reads the newspapers." Baylor turned toward Venus. "Gemma, we really have to be going. I've postponed all my morning meetings, so there's just enough time to get down to city hall. We'll say our vows and have a formal wedding later."

Her eyes darted toward Trevor. Having him there gave her all the courage she needed. "No," Venus answered firmly.

"No?" It was quite obvious that Baylor Evans was unaccustomed to hearing that word.

Venus shook her head vehemently. "I can't just run off and marry you. I don't even know you."

Baylor blew out an impatient breath. He'd apparently had enough of this.

"Yes, you do," he told her, as if insisting on it would make her remember. His eyes bored into her. "I'm Baylor."

Sensing Venus's tension and desperate to keep her at

all costs, Trevor stepped in. "She needs more than your business card, Evans."

For a moment, it looked at if Trevor and Baylor were going to lock horns. Kate rose to her feet, physically putting herself between the two men vying for the young woman in her living room.

"I know this must be difficult for you," she said, addressing her words not just to Trevor, but to Baylor, as well, "but you have to put Gemma's needs before your own." Her attention turned to Baylor. "She's been through a great deal and she needs a little time to get to know you again."

"With all due respect, Mrs. Marlowe," Baylor said, like a man who had very little respect to spare, "I don't have time for games."

"A person's emotional well-being is never a game, Mr. Evans," Kate pointed out gently, compassion in her eyes.

Faced with that, Baylor appeared to back down a fraction of an inch. "I didn't mean to imply that. You're right, of course, it's just that you can well imagine how anxious I am, in light of what's happened, to finally make her mine. I don't want to lose her again."

The bastard was playing for sympathy, Trevor thought in disgust.

"Just how did you happen to lose her the first time?" Trevor ventured. He followed his jab with a solid punch. "And why haven't we heard anything from you until now?"

Baylor answered the last question first. It was obvious that he was struggling with his temper again and that he resented having to account for his actions to anyone, let alone a stranger he felt was beneath him.

"I've been overseas the last two months."

"Well, you certainly don't look like someone who thought their fiancée was dead," Trevor said sarcastically.

Baylor's brown eyes, already somewhat small by most standards, disappeared into slits. "I have responsibilities. I can't just indulge myself with third-rate theatrics just because some buffoon thinks he and Gemma were fated to meet and he needs to challenge me."

"And how did that come about again?" Trevor pressed, refusing to let him off the hook until Baylor gave him a satisfactory answer. "The losing part," he emphasized, waiting.

Baylor addressed his answer to the police detective who had brought him here. "Gemma fell overboard while on my yacht."

"Fell, or was pushed?"

Baylor balked. "Why in heaven's name would I push her overboard and then come looking for her?"

"Looking for her after two months," Trevor pointed out. "Long after her body would have been carried off to sea, leaving you in the clear."

Baylor drew himself up to his full height—which was still less than Trevor's on a bad day. "Are you saying that I actually tried to get rid of her?"

"Your words, not mine," Trevor answered glibly.

Kate clapped her hands together, demanding attention. The two looked her way. But it was Bryan who spoke.

"Back to your corners," he ordered. "You're not going to settle anything getting in each other's faces." He turned to Baylor. "If she fell overboard, why didn't anyone try to rescue her?"

"We were on the other side of the yacht. One of my crew thought he heard a splash, but he couldn't be sure. We made our way over to the starboard side, where he thought he heard the splash, but there was no evidence that anyone had been there. I had one of my men dive, looking around the area to see if anyone had fallen. They didn't find anything. At the time, I didn't even know that the so-called missing person was Gemma. For all I knew, it was one of the crew—"

"And what, you don't save them because they're replaceable?" Trevor jeered.

Seething now, Baylor ignored him, explaining for Kate and Bryan's benefit. "My diver didn't find anyone. I chalked it up to my overactive imagination. But later that night, when I couldn't find Gemma anywhere—" he put his hand over hers in a proprietary manner that rankled Trevor "—I knew it had to have been her that I'd heard going into the water. I can't tell you how heartsick I was."

"But you still went to Europe," Trevor retorted with disgust.

Baylor's eyes turned even darker. "I already explained that there were a lot of people depending on me to do a good job."

"You still could have filed a missing-person's report," Trevor insisted. "Why didn't you?"

Baylor's annoyance was palatable and obvious. "I wasn't thinking clearly. If I was, I would have filed it immediately. Right now, her estate is in a state of limbo."

Was this proof of the man's devotion? He was in love

with her money? "Her estate?" How could this buffoon think of monetary details when he thought she'd drowned?

Baylor opened his mouth to answer, then deliberately shut it again.

"I see no reason why I should continue answering your questions. You have no right to interrogate me and I am through being polite." He turned toward Venus. "Gemma?" he said expectantly.

The name meant nothing to her. And neither did the man saying it. He meant nothing to her, but he was the cause of the uneasy, eerie feeling that filled her. It wasn't fear, it was dread. She couldn't tell if it was there because of her reluctance to give up the happiness she'd found for herself, or if something else was at the root of it. All she knew was that it made her exceedingly uncomfortable.

"We have to leave," Baylor insisted, repeating the sentence through clenched teeth.

"You're not taking her anywhere," Trevor said firmly, physically blocking access to the front door. "She's staying here."

Again Kate stepped in. She knew what Trevor had to be going through, but this wasn't about him. It was about Venus. "She needs to go back, Trevor. To be in familiar surroundings. Maybe that'll trigger her memory."

Trevor wanted to protest, to say the hell with it all and just grab Venus and run, but in his heart, he knew his step-mother was right.

Chapter Fourteen

Doing his best to steel himself, Trevor watched the woman he'd been calling Venus, the woman he wanted to spend the rest of his life with. The woman he might not be able to spend the rest of his life with, now that her past had found her.

"What do you want to do?" he asked her. It was, after all, her call, not his.

Venus took a breath, stalling. Two months ago, she knew what her answer would have been. She would have wanted to go with this man sitting in the Marlowes' living room, go with him to find out the truth and discover who she was. Half an hour ago, her answer would have been the opposite. She would have wanted to remain comfortably cocooned in her new world. A world where she felt protected, loved.

Safe.

Emotionally, she still didn't want to go. But intellectually, she knew she had to. If only to walk away from it in the end.

Squaring her shoulders, she gazed up at Trevor. The only man she'd ever loved, as far as she was concerned. The other world, in which she was engaged to this man who'd come to claim her, really didn't exist for her. When she looked at him, nothing came to mind. Baylor Evans was a stranger to her. Maybe he always would be.

But there were loose ends that needed tying and doors that needed closing. Besides, she had an uneasy feeling that not knowing would somehow come back to haunt her.

So she tried to sound as positive as possible when she told Trevor, "I want to find out who I am." To underscore their bond, she squeezed his hand.

Baylor took hold of her other hand, staking his claim. "You're Gemma King Burnett, soon to be Evans," Baylor told her impatiently. "Now can we go?"

She turned to the man who had thrown her life on its ear. Very firmly, she withdrew her hand from his. "*I* want to find out who I am," she repeated, emphasizing her own positive role in the search. "Your calling me by a different name doesn't do it. I have to see where I lived, who I interacted with, touch the things I owned—"

Baylor sighed. It was obvious that patience was not among his more highly prized virtues. "Well, can't do that here now, can you?"

Venus slanted a glance full of regret toward Trevor before answering. "No, I can't."

Her expression slashed deep into his soul. The soul he has just begun to share. The soul that was now so vulnerable.

He couldn't just let her walk away like this.

It took everything he had not to grab her hand and run, like a scene out of an old movie. Stepping in front of her before she could make a move, he asked, "Where can I reach you?"

She had no address to give him, no phone number to rattle off. That part was still very much a blank to her. Venus was forced to look toward the man on her right for answers.

Baylor seemed relieved and smug that he was in a position to break any ties Gemma had with this other man. "We'll get in contact with you once her memory comes back and she settles in."

In other words, Trevor thought, never. He couldn't just lose her now that he'd found a woman he could love the way his father loved Kate. He took his appeal to Venus. "Venus?"

"I'll call," she promised, even as Baylor hooked his arm through hers and led her away.

The detective who'd brought Baylor was on his feet, as well. It was obvious the man felt somewhat ill at ease about the way things were turning out. "Thanks for all your help." The words were addressed to the senior Marlowes. The man avoided eye contact with Trevor as he left.

Trevor turned to go, ready to follow Venus and Evans out the door, ready to mount some kind of a last-ditch protest to keep Venus from going anywhere with a man she didn't know. A man who, after all, might not be who he said he was.

But Bryan caught him by the arm, stopping him. His voice was the soul of compassion as he said, "Let her go, Trevor. She has to do this."

The agony Trevor experienced was evident in his eyes as he looked at his father. "I don't want to let her go, Dad."

Kate interceded, slipping in between her son and her husband. Her heart ached over what Trevor was going through.

"You have to, Trevor," she told him softly. "You have to let her go so she can come back."

He thought of his mother. Of promises made and broken. "What if she doesn't come back?"

It took everything she had within her for Kate to say, "Then she wasn't the woman you thought she was and she doesn't belong with you."

Trevor pressed his lips together, staving off an overflow of emotion. All very nice, neatly worded sentiments, he thought, looking at Kate. But all the words in the world didn't alleviate the kick-in-the-gut feeling he struggled with. Didn't quell the panic that rose inside him.

His temper raged, but there was no use venting. It wouldn't change anything. He heard the car pulling away outside. Venting wouldn't make her come back, he thought as his heart sank.

Trevor shoved his hands deep into his pockets, struggling to keep from smashing something. "Well, it looks like I'm going to need a salad girl again," he muttered.

Kate never hesitated. "If you're shorthanded, I can come in," she offered.

Trevor noticed the light blue-gray suit she had on. On her

days off, Kate favored jeans and crisp blouses or pullovers. This was not one of her days off. "You've got work."

"I've got a son who needs me. That's far more important. I'll reschedule my appointments," she told him, taking out her cell phone.

Trevor caught her wrist, stopping her from placing the call to her assistant. "No offense, Mom, but it's not you I need right now."

Work, he had to focus on work. The restaurant would be there long after this ache in his gut and heart would be gone. "I've got a retirement party coming in at seven. There's an awful lot I still have to do between now and seven."

Kate stopped him as he turned to leave using the back entrance. She cupped his cheek. "Are you all right, Trevor?"

At this point he was so far from all right, he doubted if he could ever navigate his way back to that state. But why tell her that? It would only upset her and there was nothing she could do about it. Nothing any of them could do about it—unless he acted crazy and followed the detective's car. He could kidnap Venus when she got out at the station. No doubt Baylor's car was parked there—and it was probably some pricey thing or even a limousine. His vintage Mustang could hardly compare to anything Evans drove.

His life of economy could hardly compare to Baylor's life, either, Trevor thought. In the end, if he truly wanted what was best for Venus, or Gemma, he silently corrected himself, then he would want her to stay with this Evans character. Because Baylor Evans could give her anything she wanted.

Unlike him.

"Yeah, I'm all right," he told Kate and tried to force a smile to his lips. He really did appreciate her concern. "Thanks for asking."

"You don't have to thank family, Trevor," she said. It wasn't the first time she'd told him that. Family came through for one another, no matter what. "I'm only a phone call away." She straightened his collar, lightly brushing her fingertips over it. "Remember that," she emphasized, looking up into his eyes. Remembering the shy boy he'd once been. Wishing she could take his pain on for him.

Trevor smiled at her, although it seemed like a sad smile to her. "I'll remember that. But like I said, I'm going to be busy for the rest of the day."

She nodded, accepting his excuse, but not giving up. "Why don't you come home for dinner afterward?" she suggested.

Picking up his briefcase, Bryan rolled his eyes. "Kate, he's around food all day—"

"Food he's cooked," Kate pointed out. "Come over and I'll cook for you, like old times," she promised. "Or we can just talk if you don't want to eat."

Trevor knew she meant well, but he still wanted to be alone. "We'll see," he answered, walking out.

That, both his parents knew, was Trevor-speak for "no."

Bryan kissed his wife quickly. He was running more than a little late and even senior partners needed to stick by the rules and set a good example. That meant getting to the office on time, or some reasonable facsimile thereof.

"He'll be fine," Bryan told her.

Kate nodded, wishing it were true. But she knew better.

"Hey, Trevor, wait up," Bryan called out to his son once he'd made it across the back-door threshold.

Impatience danced through Trevor. He really needed and wanted to be alone, to get away from everything before he said something he would regret later.

"I'm really not feeling very sociable right now, Dad," he warned.

Bryan had never been touchy-feely, although life with Kate had made him somewhat more open to that than before. But in his own way, he loved all his sons and his daughter, and wanted them to know he'd be there for them.

"You've got every right to feel that way. I just want you to know that if you need to talk, man-to-man, call me. Anytime. On my private cell," he added, underscoring his concern.

Trevor knew that his father kept two cell phones on him at all times, one for business and one in case his wife needed him. He'd taken to carrying it when Kelsey was due to be born so that Kate could reach him in time to get to the hospital. Afterward, when Kelsey was so sick as a little girl, he decided that keeping the extra phone was definitely a good idea.

"I know a little about what you're going through," Bryan added as he opened the driver's-side door to his vehicle.

His father was referring to the separation that had come just before his mother—Jill—had died in the airplane crash, Trevor thought.

"I know you do, Dad. And thanks for the concern, but I really am going to be pretty busy today."

"Then tomorrow," Bryan qualified. "Or late tonight. Anytime," he said again. With a sigh, he placed his hand on his son's shoulder. "You can get through this, Trevor."

He was glad his father thought so, Trevor thought darkly as he drove to his restaurant. Because he sure as hell didn't.

Somehow, Trevor got through the day. Putting one foot in front of the other and working on automatic pilot, he managed to hold himself together and pull off the retirement party. Several people came up to him afterward to ask about his rates and to hire him for a function.

Ordinarily, that sort of thing went a long way toward making him happy. He had carefully crafted his reputation, building it up step by step, and the heady accolades he received during the evening certainly added to it. But rather than promoting a sense of triumph and joy, the compliments and promise of future business left him completely numb.

Remembering to smile, Trevor hardly heard any of the words.

All he heard was her voice in his head.

Venus laughing, talking, teasing him. Her voice was louder than anything he heard around him until it drowned everything else out.

It was slowly, steadily driving him crazy.

"Hey, boss man," Emilio called out for the second time, trying to snare his attention, "is Venus going to be in tomorrow?" As he asked the casual question, Emilio stripped off the apron he had wrapped around his middle. Set to toss it aside, he hesitated, then neatly folded it over the back of a chair.

Although such a stickler for efficiency, for neatness, for logic, Trevor let his emotions rip. The answer came out on a wave of molten lava before he could stop himself. "No," Trevor barked.

No excuse had been given for Venus's conspicuous absence. She was just "out." Everyone naturally assumed she was under Trevor's protective wing and asked no questions. Still, there were those who wouldn't hold their tongues—like Emilio—and had a desire to know the whereabouts of their newest staff member.

Trevor had made himself deliberately unavailable to Emilio for no other reason than because he didn't want to answer any questions about Venus's situation. But now it was unavoidable.

"Is she sick?" Emilio cajoled.

Trevor curbed the urge to walk away. "She's gone," he snapped.

"Gone?" His dark eyebrows formed one concerned line. "What do you mean, 'she's gone'?"

"Gone," Trevor repeated, raising his voice. "As in not here. Gone, as in not coming back." He gritted his teeth together. Even his teeth ached, he thought. Everything ached, as if he'd been skewered. "Gone as in gone."

Emilio shook his head, obviously not happy about the news. "What d'you say to her to get her ticked off at you?"

He liked Emilio, relied on Emilio, but right now, he

just wanted the man out of his face and out of his business. "You're crossing that line again," Trevor growled at him.

"With all due respect, Trevor, the hell with that line of yours. I'm trying to get down to the bottom of something way more important than lines here." His eyes held Trevor's. "Why isn't Venus coming back?"

Taking hold of his arm, Trevor pulled the smaller man over to a far less populated side of the kitchen. "You want to know? Okay, I'll tell you.

"Because some guy," he continued with more than a little loathing, "in a suit that cost more than that exclusive espresso machine we imported from Italy showed up at my parents' house and said she was his fiancée."

Surprise, concern and then suspicion washed over Emilio's expressive face. He winced. "Ouch. And you believed him?"

It wasn't as if he wanted to, Trevor thought. But he wasn't about to share that with anyone. The only one he shared thoughts like that with were his brothers—and Venus. "Didn't see a reason not to."

"Did Venus know this guy?"

That was what made it twice as difficult to deal with. "No."

Again Emilio shook his head, this time in disbelief. "Seems to me that when the former love of your life comes walking back into it, there should have been some kind of nudge toward remembering. Is that what happened?" he asked. "Did she show any signs that things were coming back to her?"

"No," Trevor rasped. The words all tasted appallingly stale in his mouth and it was enough to make him want to gag. He didn't want to talk about this anymore and he knew that Emilio could go on for hours on nothing. How much more could he talk when there *was* an actual topic of dissent?

Trevor tried to distance himself from what he was saying and found that he couldn't. "She's a big girl. She can look out for herself. Besides, she knows where I live. She knows my number. She can get in contact with me if she wants to."

The words were no sooner out of his mouth than the phone in his pocket rang.

Trevor all but jumped out of his skin.

His fingers wrapped around the phone and he yanked it out of his pocket, flipping it open with his thumb as he pulled.

"Hello?"

There was no one on the other end, just a dial tone. He glanced down at the caller ID screen, but it identified the caller as simply Private.

A wrong number, he thought, disappointment floating through him. He flipped the phone closed so hard, the shell threatened to break.

Emilio began to tread on eggshells. "Want me to lock up?" he offered.

Trevor definitely didn't like the pity he saw in the other man's dark brown eyes. The last thing he wanted was to be anyone's object of pity.

"No. Go home, Emilio," he ordered.

"You've got my number if you want to talk," the assistant chef called back as he walked away.

Why did everyone think he wanted to talk? Trevor thought darkly. He didn't want to talk, he wanted to hit something. Anything.

To hit someone.

To hit that sleek, every-hair-in-place buffoon who'd trespassed, uninvited, into his life and taken Venus out of it.

Taken the sun out of it.

But he couldn't hit the man, not without undoubtedly incurring an arrest and, most likely, a lawsuit. The man seemed like the type to indulge in petty lawsuits.

So, in order to survive, he'd focused on one of the few things he could do: putting the kitchen to bed.

He did it slowly because he figured it was going to be a long, long night. And he no longer had a place to be.

Chapter Fifteen

Emilio cleared his throat. When Trevor looked at him absently, Emilio nodded toward the large jar that he was holding. "That's the honey."

His mind admittedly in a fog, as it had been these last few days, Trevor blinked, trying to focus. It didn't work. "What?"

"In your hand." Emilio tapped the jar in Trevor's hand. "You're holding a jar of honey." He did his best to treat lightly the situation that had everyone in the kitchen concerned. Nobody wanted to insult the boss. "Have you changed the recipe for the spaghetti sauce without telling me?"

Trevor glanced down at his hand as if to verify what Emilio had just pointed out. With a sigh, he returned the half-filled jar to the counter, putting it down with a thud. His mind had drifted off. Again. Just the way it had for the last six days. He needed to shake it off. This daze that had him sleepwalking through his life.

"No, I did not change the recipe," he answered tersely.

"That's good to know because the thought of honey in spaghetti sauce—" Emilio didn't complete the sentence. The shiver he gave conveyed his thoughts on the matter. And then, because he'd never been one to hold his tongue for long, Emilio asked, "How long are you going to let this go on?"

"'This'?" Trevor echoed. There was a dangerous note in his voice that would have warned a man of lesser courage to back off.

But Emilio obviously ignored it. "Yeah. You here, her there." His customary grin was gone, replaced by a look of concern. "Don't you think it's time to bridge the gap?"

Trevor resisted the urge to tell his assistant to mind his own business. He started chopping an onion. "It's not up to me."

Emilio had always believed that every man was captain of his own destiny. The comment didn't sit well with him. "Then who's it up to?"

Trevor tilted the cutting board over the pot of sauce, sending the diced onion pieces into the red, bubbling sea. "Her."

Emilio raised his eyebrows. "She's supposed to come after you?"

"Not after me, *to* me." Slamming the cutting board down on the large metal table, he made more noise than he'd intended. Trevor lowered his voice. "I'm not the one who left."

Emilio shook his head, compassion entering his features. "Trevor, you're a great boss and a fantastic chef, but what you don't know about women could fill the Grand Canyon."

Everyone knew that Emilio loved the ladies and they loved him back. To Trevor, it had always seemed like rather an empty existence, partying all the time without that one particular someone who mattered beside you. He didn't want Emilio's pity.

Picking up a large wooden spoon, Trevor blended the onion deep into the sauce. A flurry of mozzarella cheese came next, disappearing into the sauce like the diced onion.

"Oh?"

"Yeah, 'oh.'" Emilio moved to get into Trevor's line of sight. "A woman wants to have a guy come after her, make her feel that she's worth the effort, that the guy will fight to have her in his life."

Trevor frowned. He could just hear his sister's reaction to that philosophy. "That's stereotypical and sexist."

"That's life," Emilio insisted with feeling. "I've got five sisters, remember? Not one of them is happy calling all the shots. Don't get me wrong, they all like to manipulate," he quickly interjected, "but they also like the idea of being rescued."

Trevor stopped stirring and looked at him. "Rescued," he echoed.

The grin on Emilio's face was worthy of a man who had just shared the secrets of the universe. "That's the word. Rescued. That other guy's not any good for her, I don't care how many expensive suits he owns."

"Rescued," Trevor repeated again. Clearly his assistant wasn't getting enough sleep because of the wild life he led. "From a billionaire who could give her anything she ever dreamed of."

The small frown on Emilio's lips indicated that he felt Trevor had missed the point. "From a guy who's a control freak. I did a little research on that Baylor Evans guy and besides being a workaholic, he also likes his women to be available whenever he wants them."

"What women? He wants Venus—Gemma—to marry him." Trevor still couldn't get his mouth around the other name. To him, she was Venus. The name suited her.

"I don't know about her, but I was talking about his fancy women." The smile on Emilio's face was nothing short of wicked. "The ones Mr. Billionaire can't bring home to mother."

"How would you know this?" Trevor asked.

The wicked smile turned smugly secretive. "Hey, there are ways to find things out. You just gotta know where to look, who to ask."

Billionaire or not, the man was a lowlife—just as he'd pegged him, Trevor thought.

"You'd be rescuing her from a pretty miserable marriage—" Emilio was saying.

His mind was drifting again. Trevor forced himself to focus. "Maybe it's what she wants." In any case, he was done, he was moving on, he silently insisted. Trevor felt Emilio's dark eyes boring into him expectantly. "Look, she hasn't called. I've had the cell phone on me 24/7 and nothing."

"So? Don't stand on ceremony," Emilio insisted. "You're making a mistake…in the kitchen—" he nodded at the honey jar on the counter "—and in your life."

They'd closed twenty minutes ago. He was just trying to get a jump start on the spaghetti sauce for tomorrow's featured item on the menu. He'd been told that people drove for two hours just to eat his sauce. They'd stop coming if they sampled the dish after he'd emptied the contents of that jar of honey into it.

But he'd be damned if he was going to admit it.

"Go home, Emilio. Don't you have someone waiting for you?" What was the most recent girl's name? "Susannah?" he guessed.

"Shirley."

Trevor nodded. He got back to work. "Knew it started with *S.*"

As Trevor went to another stove, Emilio dogged his tracks, not about to give up easily. "Go to her. Everyone here will thank you for it. You haven't been the same since she left."

Trevor wanted to protest that he'd been exactly the same, but he knew it was a lie. He hadn't been the same. He'd felt lost and out of sorts, and yesterday, when Mike called to ask how he was doing, he'd all but taken his older brother's head off. That wasn't like him at all.

He used to be the patient one, the easygoing one, as his stepmother pointed out when she called about twenty minutes later. News traveled fast on the Marlowe grapevine. Even that had irritated him and he had never, ever gotten irritated because of anything Kate said to him.

Emilio was right, he thought, turning off the heat beneath the pot. He'd let the sauce simmer a few minutes, then put it into the refrigerator. In the interim, he'd put away the few leftovers from tonight's menu into the freezer. First thing tomorrow, the leftovers were going to St. Anne's Homeless Shelter.

But as for him, the second he finished locking up, he would talk to Travis, who had some connections at the police force. Maybe he could find out where Venus had gone. Not just find out where she'd gone, but bring her back from there, as well. He didn't care what "Gemma" did, but Venus was coming back with him. He might as well admit it, he needed her and there was no use pretending that he didn't.

The hell with being noble and doing what was best for her. Marrying someone like Baylor Evans *wasn't* best for her. Evans could never love her the way he did and there were more important things than money in this world.

There was love.

And damn it, he wasn't giving up his, not without a fight.

Trevor hit the main switch that controlled the kitchen lights, turning them off. He began to make his way to the back office, to make sure that the computer was shut down for the night before he left. Now that he'd decided what to do, he was anxious to get rolling.

When he heard the voice, he thought he was hallucinating.

"They'll go bad by morning if you leave them out."

If he turned around, she wouldn't be there, he silently told himself. Just like the other times he'd thought he heard Venus's voice, only to discover that it was just his mind working overtime. Taunting him.

"The salad is the first step to a memorable dining experience," the soft voice went on to say. "Isn't that what you told me?"

Frozen in place, his very shoulder muscles ached. Okay, Trevor reasoned, he was either certifiable, or she was here.

He swung around, half-afraid he was losing his mind, fervently praying that he'd see her standing there—even if seeing her meant that he *had* lost his mind.

Adrenaline drummed wildly through his system.

It was her.

Venus.

She was standing in his kitchen before the butcher-block table where he'd absently left half a tray of side salads. In his haste to finish, he'd forgotten all about them.

Moving forward, Venus glanced down at the small plates. "I see you've replaced me."

He was afraid to breathe. Afraid that if he did, he'd wake up. And she'd be gone. "Not possible," he murmured.

As he watched, her lips curved into a smile that shot straight to his gut, further immobilizing him. "Because I was so good, or so bad?"

Okay, if he didn't breathe, he was going to pass out. Ever so slowly, he pulled air into his lungs. She was still there.

"Because you were you. Unique." He drew nearer,

not fully conscious of the process of putting one foot in front of the other. Just desperate to be close to her.

Her perfume filled his head. Another trick of the mind? "Is it really you?"

Her smile widened as her eyes met his. "As far as I know."

"And who are you?" Was she Gemma? Or his Venus?

The smile turned mysterious. *Eat your heart out, Mona Lisa.* "A question for the ages."

Her answer told him what he wanted to know. "You remember."

She nodded her head slowly. "Everything. My name, my isolated childhood. Baylor. Everything," she repeated.

"And you've come to say goodbye," he guessed, feeling heartsick. What other conclusion could there be? On the one hand was a life in which she could have everything she ever wanted or aspired to, on the other was working for a living. Not much of a contest there, he thought cynically.

"No, I've come to say hello," she replied, measuring out each word as if it was cast in gold.

Trevor was afraid to hope. He wanted it spelled out for him. "What does that mean?"

"It means," she informed him patiently, "that I've given up waiting for you to come riding up on a white charger to rescue me from the pompous ass I was engaged to."

If he was dreaming, he hoped he'd never wake up. But even asleep, he needed things to make sense.

"If he's such a pompous ass, why were you engaged to him?"

Another question for the ages, she thought. "Didn't know any better." Actually, there was more to it than that. "I thought all men were more or less alike. I lived among very self-centered, privileged people with my father as a male role model." She toyed with one of the salads, turning the plate around and around as she talked. "Not to speak ill of the dead, but Hayden Burnett was the king of the self-centered people."

He knew very little about the world she came from. Until recently, it had nothing to do with him. "He's dead?"

She nodded. "Died of a heart attack last year. Baylor was his successor. At the bank and, apparently, in my life." A great deal had come flooding back to her in a very short time. Even though they were her memories, she was still sorting them all out. And seeing things in a very different light. "I don't blame him for what he is, he can't help it. Apparently, he didn't have any good role models, either. His father was never home, too busy working, and his mother tried to drown herself one martini at a time." Drawing closer, she smiled up into his eyes. "Not like you." She thought about that for a moment. "Although I suspect that you probably would have been you even if wolves had raised you."

Oh God, she was back. This wasn't a dream or a hallucination, she was really back. Tension instantly evaporated from his body, leaving him drained and very, very happy. "They'd have to be nice wolves, otherwise they'd have eaten me."

She nodded, a grin struggling to take over her lips. "Good point."

Slipping his arms around her waist, he drew her to him. "I was going to come to rescue you, you know."

Venus lifted her head and looked up into his eyes. "Oh? When?"

He nodded back at the refrigerator, as if it could bear him out. "Right after I closed up tonight."

She glanced over her shoulder at the neglected tray. "And left the tray of salads out."

"My mind wasn't on salads," he told her, "it was on finding you."

She did believe him. Trevor wouldn't lie. "I guess I took the work out of that, huh?"

He cupped her face, glorying in being able to touch her after nights of yearning to do just that. "So you've left him?"

She nodded. She'd told Baylor in no uncertain terms that he was never going to marry her—or her substantial bank account. "Shed him like the last unwanted ten pounds on a diet."

If he wasn't so happy, he could have actually felt a little sorry for the worthless scum, Trevor mused. "What did he say?"

"That I'd regret it." Baylor had said a lot of other things too, harsh, hateful things that didn't bear repeating and only confirmed that she'd made the right choice.

"You might." It killed him to say it, but it was true. He wanted her to be very, very sure. "I can't give you the lifestyle you're used to."

Money had been important enough to her once, but not anymore. Not after she'd seen life on the other side of a banking institution. "Maybe not," she allowed, "but I can."

He wasn't sure he followed her. "What?"

He was so adorable when he was confused, she thought. God, but she had missed him. Missed his eyes, his hair, the scent of his cologne, the scent of his sweat. Most of all, she missed his smile.

"Baylor Evans didn't want me because he was head over heels in love with me, Trevor. I come with connections, a pedigree and, most of all, money."

It didn't seem to him that Evans needed money. "He's a billionaire."

"A little overexaggerated," she corrected. "Besides, billionaires like money, too. Sometimes more than the rest of us."

Us. He combed his fingers through her hair, framing her face. A tiny part of him was still afraid he'd suddenly wake up. "So now you've come over to my side."

Her smile encompassed her eyes. "If that proposal is still open."

How could she even ask that? "You know it is." Unable to hold himself in check any longer, he kissed her. Hard. But then, even though he wanted to continue, to take it up to the next level and the next, he drew back. There were things he had to know. "You've got your full memory back?"

She threaded her arms around his neck as she nodded. "Came back to me with thunder and lightning the minute I saw my house." She smiled. "You don't forget a nine-thousand-square-foot 'home.' Mausoleum is more like it," she admitted ruefully. It was where she had grown up, but the place had never been a home. Her mother had died when she was very young, leaving her to be raised by strangers who cared for her because they were paid to do so. Her father was hardly ever around—except to criticize her. "I also remembered that I came to the conclusion that I was making a terrible mistake, agreeing to marry Baylor."

He wondered how much she actually did remember. "What happened that night I found you?"

She smiled up into his eyes, pressing her body against his. "I was reborn."

He could feel himself responding to her. Wanting her. It was hard to hold himself in check. "Before that. Do you remember how you got into the water? Did you jump in?"

She shook her head. She wasn't that foolhardy and reckless. "After I realized my mistake, I tried to get into a lifeboat in order to row back to shore. Baylor isn't the kind of man you reason with—or to take what he considered humiliation well. He has a nasty temper. And my leaving him at the altar made him look like an even bigger idiot than he already was. But I slipped, lost my hold on the ropes, not to mention my footing, and hit the water.

"After that, I don't remember much." She shrugged. Whether or not she remembered didn't matter. What mattered was that her life began the moment Trevor rescued her. "I guess survival instincts took over and I started swimming for shore."

"Wouldn't it have been easier just to call for help from someone on the yacht?"

"There was a party going on. I doubt if anyone would have heard me." That was how she'd managed to slip away in the first place. Baylor had invited two hundred of his "closest" friends. "The music was too loud for anyone to hear me."

There was still one glaring question left. "Why didn't Baylor file a missing-person's report on you right away?"

His actions, she thought, were very typical of the man and, until she'd met Trevor, she would have thought it was typical of all men. "It was…inconvenient, I guess. He was supposed to go to Europe on business right after the ceremony. He considered it a 'working' honeymoon. He assumed I either fell—or jumped. The first would get him bogged down in red tape, the second would be a blow to his ego because if I jumped, that meant I preferred taking my chances with the sea and the possibility of a watery grave to marrying him. That would have been too humiliating for him to admit to, to say the least. He said he did have some of his crew search for me, but it was dark and—" Her slim shoulders rose and fell in a careless shrug.

"So why did he finally file?"

The answer was simplicity personified. And so very Baylor. "Because he's in my will and in order to collect, I had to be declared legally dead."

"Some guy you picked to fall in love with," Trevor snorted.

"I didn't pick him," she admitted. "I was just indifferent and maybe a bit of a snob myself." In a way, she would have deserved what she got—but life had given her a second chance with Trevor. "There was all that prestige and the bank to think of."

"What about the bank?"

She smiled. "I have the controlling fifty-one shares, thanks to my father. For now, Baylor is the best man for the job—rotten human being, but excellent banking executive. Besides, I can always have him fired if he doesn't perform well." She looked up at Trevor. She wanted to feel his lips on her again. To have him make love with her again. It had been far too long. "I don't want to talk about him anymore."

Trevor tucked her soft form against his, resting his fingertips against the swell of her hips. "What do you want to talk about?"

"Were you really going to come after me tonight?" *Lie to me. Say yes. I'll believe you.*

"Yes."

He said it with such sincerity. She believed him. "How did you know how to find me?"

"Travis has a couple of friends on the police force," he told her. "I was thinking of having one of them access your driver's license. Your current address had to be on it."

She nodded. That made sense. "Simple plan."

"Those are usually the best." He could feel his heart singing. "Nothing wrong with simplicity."

"No," she agreed, "there certainly isn't." She pretended that she didn't want to jump his bones right this minute. "So, aside from leaving salads out overnight, what else have you been up to?"

"I can't remember," he told her honestly. "My days and nights were filled with missing you."

Right back at you. She wiggled into place beside him. "You don't have to miss me anymore."

"Not ever again," he swore. "Marry me."

She did her best to look innocent as she asked, "How do I know you're not marrying me for my ability to make salads?"

Brushing his lips against hers, he laughed. "I'd marry you if you couldn't boil water."

She sighed, relieved. A part of her had been afraid that he wouldn't take her back. That she'd wounded his pride by going off with Baylor, even if it had been for all the right reasons. "Then I guess it must be love."

"Let me take the guesswork out of it for you." With a sweep of his hand, he sent the salads and the tray that held them onto the floor. The table was now cleared. And ready for them. He planted her on top of the table.

She kept her arms around his neck. "You really do love me."

"Forever and always," he whispered.

Her eyes were gleaming as she told him, "I can live with that."

"Yeah. Me, too." Each word was separated by a long pause during which time he kissed her.

And then he stopped talking altogether. There were more important things to do. And he did them.

Epilogue

She'd been here before. Looking into a mirror, seeing herself as a bride, just like this. But back then, she'd been wearing a designer wedding gown fit for an heiress to an empire. Fit for a symbol. The money the gown had cost would have fed a third-world village well for six months, if not longer. She'd given the gown away to a secondhand store, refusing to even entertain the idea of wearing it today, on this, the most important day of her life.

No, Venus amended, the second most important day of her life. The first had been the night she had met Trevor. Because if Trevor hadn't come into her life just when he did, she wouldn't have been reborn, wouldn't have been this unbelievably happy—never mind that she would have drowned. The woman she had been had only managed to sleepwalk through life.

The woman she was now savored every sight, every sound, every feeling that came her way. And, most of all, she savored the fact that she was going to be Trevor's wife. Not only was she marrying a wonderful man, but along with him, she was getting the first real family she'd ever known. A family that already cared more about her than the one she'd been born into.

"Tears?" Kate asked, slipping into the back office of the restaurant where her about-to-be daughter-in-law had chosen to change into her strapless, floor-length wedding gown.

Venus automatically took the handkerchief that Kate held out to her and nodded as she dabbed at her eyes. "I didn't realize you actually could cry when you were happy," she said with a sniff.

Taking back the handkerchief, Kate carefully wiped away a small dark smudge beneath one of Venus's eyes. "Yes, but don't cry too much. You don't want to spoil all that lovely makeup before the photographer finishes immortalizing you." Kate stood back as far as the small, crammed space allowed her to, taking in the full view. "You look beautiful."

Venus took a breath to steady the jangle of nerves, nerves of excitement, of anticipation. "I feel beautiful," she replied.

Kate smiled. "Love can do that to you." Strains of the wedding march were heard, starting to play in the distance. Time to go.

Just as she thought it, there was a soft rap on the door.

"Come in," Venus called out just as Kate finished smoothing out the edges of her veil.

Bryan peeked in. In lieu of a father, or walking down the aisle by herself, she'd asked him to give her away. He'd beamed as he agreed.

"Ready?" he asked.

The answer escaped before she even thought to say the words. "Oh, yes."

"Then let's get this show on the road," he urged, presenting his arm to her.

"No butterflies? No last-minute escape plans?" Travis teased as he leaned against the doorjamb of the supply closet. His eyes were on Trevor. Kelsey was busy making and then straightening his tie.

"Why would I want to escape?" Trevor asked. "I've been waiting for Venus all my life."

"So it's official, then? She wants us to call her Venus instead of Gemma?" Trent queried, standing on the other side of the doorjamb. Between him and Travis, they framed the doorway like identical bookends.

"She *is* Venus," Trevor replied. "Gemma is just someone she used to be." He smiled to himself. No matter what her birth certificate said, she would always be Venus to him. That she agreed and actually wanted him to call her that only made him that much more sure that they belonged together.

He had no idea how he'd managed to get so lucky, but he wasn't about to rock the boat by wondering about it.

He was just eternally grateful that she had come into his life and that something had drawn him to the beach that evening.

The same beach where they were now getting married.

"Hey, stop fussing over his tie and let's get a move on, unless you want to miss the sunset," Mike warned, adding his body to the already crowded area.

Kelsey released her fingers from Trevor's tie just in time. Half a second longer and she would have undone it again. Trevor turned quickly in response to his older brother's urging and immediately headed out the door. The whole idea behind getting married on the beach was to have the sunset as a backdrop. He wanted to make this as memorable for Venus as possible.

As for him, it would have been memorable even if they were to say their vows crammed inside a cardboard box beneath the San Diego Freeway overpass. The memorable part would be saying "I do" to the only woman he'd really ever loved.

Taking his position by the priest, with Mike acting as his best man, Trevor stood with the sun directly behind him. It looked like a red ball of fire preparing to slowly sink into the ocean. His attention was fixed on Venus as she came to him, lighting up his heart with every step she took.

Even as the music played and the words that would pledge them to one another before God and the state of California still waited to be said, he mouthed, "I love you," to her.

Trevor smiled broadly as he saw her lips silently move to echo the words back to him.

In his heart, they were already married.

* * * * *

Don't miss Marie Ferrarella's next romance,
COLTON'S SECRET SERVICE,
available September 2008
from Silhouette Romantic Suspense.

The Colton family is back!
Enjoy a sneak preview of
COLTON'S SECRET SERVICE
by Marie Ferrarella,
part of THE COLTONS: FAMILY FIRST *miniseries.*
Available from Silhouette Romantic Suspense
in September 2008.

He cautioned himself to be leery. He was human and he'd been conned before. But never by anyone nearly so attractive. Never by anyone he'd felt so attracted to.

In her defense, Nick supposed that Georgie could actually be telling him the truth. That she was a victim in all this. He had his people back in California checking her out, to make sure she was who she said she was and had, as she claimed, not even been near a computer but on the road these last few months that the threats had been made.

In the meantime, he was doing his own checking out. Up close and exceedingly personal. So personal he could feel his blood stirring.

It had been a long time since he'd thought of himself as anything other than a law enforcement agent of one type or other. But Georgeann Grady made him remember that beneath the oaths he had taken and his devotion to duty, there beat the heart of a man.

A man who'd been far too long without the touch of a woman.

He watched as the light from the fireplace caressed the outline of Georgie's small, trim, jean-clad body as she moved about the rustic living room that could have easily come off the set of a Hollywood Western. Except that it was genuine.

As genuine as she claimed to be?

Something inside him hoped so.

He wasn't supposed to be taking sides. His only interest in being here was to guarantee Senator Joe Colton's safety as the latter continued to make his bid for the presidency. Everything else was supposed to be secondary, but, Nick had to silently admit, that was just a wee bit hard to remember right now.

Earlier, before she'd put her precocious handful of a daughter to bed, Georgie had fed his appetite by whipping up some kind of a delicious concoction out of the vegetables she'd pulled from her garden. Vegetables that, by all rights, should have been withered and dried. She'd mentioned that a friend came by on occasion to weed and tend it. Still, it surprised him that somehow she'd managed to make something mouthwatering out of it.

Almost as mouthwatering as she looked to him right at this moment.

Again, he was reminded of the appetite that hadn't been fed, hadn't been satisfied.

And wasn't going to be, Nick sternly told himself. At least not now. Maybe later, when things took on a more definite shape and all the questions in his head were answered to his satisfaction, there would be time to explore this feeling. This woman. But not now.

Damn it.

"Sorry about the lack of light," Georgie said, breaking into his train of thought as she turned around to face him. If she noticed the way he was looking at her, she gave no indication. "But I don't see a point in paying for electricity if I'm not going to be here. Besides, Emmie really enjoys camping out. She likes roughing it."

"And you?" Nick asked, moving closer to her, so close that a whisper would have trouble fitting in. "What do you like?"

The very breath stopped in Georgie's throat as she looked up at him.

"I think you've got a fair shot of guessing that one," she told him softly.

* * * * *

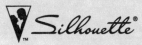

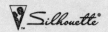

SPECIAL EDITION

HEART OF STONE
by
DIANA PALMER

On sale September.

SAVE $1.⁰⁰ OFF

**the Silhouette Special Edition® novel
HEART OF STONE on sale
September 2008, when you purchase
2 Silhouette Special Edition® books.**

*Available wherever books are sold, including most
bookstores, supermarkets, drugstores and discount stores.*

Coupon expires December 31, 2008. Redeemable at participating
retail outlets in the U.S. only. Limit one coupon per customer.

U.S. RETAILERS: Harlequin Enterprises Limited will pay the face value of this coupon plus
8¢ if submitted by customer for this specified product only. Any other use constitutes fraud.
Coupon is nonassignable. Void if taxed, prohibited or restricted by law. Consumer must pay
any government taxes. Void if copied. For reimbursement submit coupons and proof of sales
directly to Harlequin Enterprises Limited, P.O. Box 880478, El Paso, TX 88588-0478, U.S.A.
Cash value 1/100 cents. Limit one coupon per customer. Valid in the U.S. only.

5 65373 00076 2   (8100) 0 11556

SSECPNUS0808

Silhouette

SPECIAL EDITION

HEART OF STONE
by
DIANA PALMER

On sale September.

SAVE $1.⁰⁰ OFF

the Silhouette Special Edition® novel
HEART OF STONE on sale
**September 2008, when you purchase
2 Silhouette Special Edition® books.**

*Available wherever books are sold, including most
bookstores, supermarkets, drugstores and discount stores.*

Coupon expires December 31, 2008. Redeemable at participating
retail outlets in Canada only. Limit one coupon per customer.

52608458

SSECPNCDN0808

REQUEST YOUR FREE BOOKS!

2 FREE NOVELS PLUS 2 FREE GIFTS!

SPECIAL EDITION®

Life, Love and Family!

YES! Please send me 2 FREE Silhouette Special Edition® novels and my 2 FREE gifts (gifts are worth about $10). After receiving them, if I don't wish to receive any more books, I can return the shipping statement marked "cancel." If I don't cancel, I will receive 6 brand-new novels every month and be billed just $4.24 per book in the U.S. or $4.99 per book in Canada, plus 25¢ shipping and handling per book and applicable taxes, if any*. That's a savings of at least 15% off the cover price! I understand that accepting the 2 free books and gifts places me under no obligation to buy anything. I can always return a shipment and cancel at any time. Even if I never buy another book from Silhouette, the two free books and gifts are mine to keep forever.

235 SDN EEYU   335 SDN EEY6

Name	(PLEASE PRINT)

Address	Apt. #

City	State/Prov.	Zip/Postal Code

Signature (if under 18, a parent or guardian must sign)

Mail to the Silhouette Reader Service:
IN U.S.A.: P.O. Box 1867, Buffalo, NY 14240-1867
IN CANADA: P.O. Box 609, Fort Erie, Ontario L2A 5X3

Not valid to current subscribers of Silhouette Special Edition books.

Want to try two free books from another line?
Call 1-800-873-8635 or visit www.morefreebooks.com.

* Terms and prices subject to change without notice. N.Y. residents add applicable sales tax. Canadian residents will be charged applicable provincial taxes and GST. Offer not valid in Quebec. This offer is limited to one order per household. All orders subject to approval. Credit or debit balances in a customer's account(s) may be offset by any other outstanding balance owed by or to the customer. Please allow 4 to 6 weeks for delivery. Offer available while quantities last.

Your Privacy: Silhouette is committed to protecting your privacy. Our Privacy Policy is available online at www.eHarlequin.com or upon request from the Reader Service. From time to time we make our lists of customers available to reputable third parties who may have a product or service of interest to you. If you would prefer we not share your name and address, please check here. ☐

SSE08R

Silhouette *Desire*

Billionaires and Babies

MAUREEN CHILD

BABY BONANZA

Newly single mom Jenna Baker has only one thing on her mind: child support for her twin boys. Ship owner and carefree billionaire Nick Falco discovers he's a daddy—brought on by a night of passion a year ago. Nick may be ready to become a father, but is he ready to become a groom when he discovers the passion that still exists between him and Jenna?

**Available September
wherever books are sold.**

Always Powerful, Passionate and Provocative.

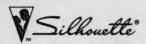
Silhouette®

COMING NEXT MONTH

SSECNM0808